PRESENTS

BY

KATHRYN C. KELLY

Bounty by Kathryn C. Kelly
Mayhem Makers Series
Published by Makin Groceries Media
24200 SW Freeway, Suite 402, Box #353
Rosenberg, TX 77471
www.katkelwriter.com
www.deathdwellersmc.com

© 2025 Kathryn C. Kelly
© 2025 Cover Design CT Creations
© 2025 Cover Image Period Images

Bounty
Mayhem Makers Series
By Kathryn C. Kelly

All rights reserved. This book or any portion thereof may not be reproduced or used in any manner whatsoever without the express written permission of the publisher except for the use of brief quotations in a book review.

Manufactured in the United States of America

This is a work of fiction. The characters, incidents and dialogue in this book are of the author's imagination and are not to be construed as real. Any resemblance to actual events or persons, living or dead, is completely coincidental.

Author's Note

Though the Motorcycles, Mobsters, and Mayhem Book Signing is an actual event, the plot of *Bounty* is fiction and completely made up. Nothing of the sort has transpired at any of the signings.

I dedicate this book to my three beautiful girls. Laugh always. Love hard. Pray often. Dance as much as possible.

My darling Kate, words cannot express how much I admire you. You're a joy and an inspiration. I'm so proud of you. Thank you for your comments and your brainstorming. Thank you for your side-eye when I went off the chain. Thank you for being you. Though you're the middle, I decided to put you first this time. Otherwise, you would've been in between, either by age or by alphabet.

My dear Zoey, my sugar monkey. My first born. You amaze me every day. You're a wonderful wife, an upstanding woman, and an exceptional mother.

My sweet Alegra, my baby girl, as you forge your own path in the world, I pray each day that all your dreams come true and your hard work pays off. You have brains and talent. I know you will go far.

I also dedicate this book to my mom, Memaw Kelly.

Momma, you're the foundation of our family. I have always been proud to have you as my mother. Thank you for all your sacrifices, support, and encouragement.

I love you all so much.

BOUNTY

MAYHEM MAKERS

Effie

Last-minute changes were never good, especially when the heart was set on something completely different. Partying like a rock star while Mom was away, for instance. Escaping her watchful eye at a friend's house and getting lit all weekend long.

Alas, that wasn't to be. My older sister, forever an irresponsible wretch, backed out on helping our mother with her book signing. Specifically, Motorcycles, Mobsters, and Mayhem in Austin. It was Mom's favorite event, one she looked forward to whenever it took place. Since confirming her attendance, she hadn't stopped ranting and raving about her excitement.

Cassie went with Mom in her first year as an attending author. I joined Mom the next time. We had a deal. One year I'd go, and one year Cassie went. By right, this event should've been Cassie's turn, but she backed out two days ago because of a big fight with jerk boy. Also known as her longtime loser boyfriend and the *lurve* of her life.

My sister could've done so much better than him. It was a sentiment echoed by our parents, because, shocker, jerk boy was a jerk. However, once I entered adulthood, I gave up trying to save her from the asshole.

Her life. Her choice. I was the last person she'd listen to, anyway.

Sighing, I dropped another dick lollipop in a cellophane bag and set it aside on the pile I'd amassed on my desk. I was stuffing Mom's swag bags with the lollipops, little dick soaps, trading cards with characters from her most popular book, beaded keychains with a miniature cover of that book, a pen with her name, her business card, personalized magnets, stickers, and lip balm.

Whether I went with Mom to her signings, stuffing her swag bags always fell to me. Cassie never concerned herself with trivial details and Mom had a bajillion other things to do.

Once I finished stuffing the bags, I'd grab a bite to eat and bottled water, then slap stickers with Mom's name in curlicue and tie each bag with a ribbon.

Half an hour later, I finished stuffing bag number two hundred. This shit took up my entire morning. Shoving my chair back, I stood and stretched, pleased with myself.

Stacks of books, boxes of mugs, tote bags, and T-shirts lined the floor of my normally neat room. Mom used a color scheme from each room in our house for her book covers. My cheery yellow and white décor didn't suit a dramatic title like *The Biker in Me*, so she inverted those colors. Yellow became blue and white turned black. My lacy curtains and bedspread translated to dark smoke in her mind.

It worked—that book hit several bestseller lists.

I started toward my door, but an abandoned trading card sat at the edge of my dresser. When I grabbed the stack Mom left there, I must've overlooked this one.

Slice's image taunted me. I bit my lip, shoved a hand in the pocket of my fluffy jacket, and immediately abandoned the idea of checking for a message from him. Or sending another one. Whatever it took for him to respond.

I laid the card back on my dresser and sat on the edge of my bed, needing a moment to gather myself and overcome my disappointment and despair over how my friendship with the biker had turned out.

Once the upcoming signing ended and I returned home, I'd decide if I wanted to demand answers about why he ghosted me or if I'd just forget him as he seemed to have forgotten me.

Mom pushed open my door and peeked in. "Are the swag bags finished?"

"I just have to cut the ribbon, tie the bags, and add your stickers, Mom." I pushed excitement into my voice. If I didn't think about Slice, I was fine. "I'll be finished by dinner."

"Get it done ASAP, love," Mom huffed. "I don't want to leave later than planned."

We weren't leaving until tomorrow, but I didn't point that out.

"Slice will probably beat us there," she announced. "We're lugging all this stuff in a big old SUV, and he'll be on that beautiful machine."

"What?"

Slice was going? That changed everything.

Mom stepped fully into my room, still in her writer's uniform of yoga pants and sweatshirt, her curls piled on top of her head in a messy bun. When she ran errands, she added socks, small earrings, and tennis shoes to her getup. She insisted it was a sufficient outfit, and dressing fancier was unnecessary. I disagreed. The minute I discovered I'd accompany her, determination to doll her up for the signing filled me.

As her assistant, she also gave me the responsibility of packing our bags. Her new, Effie-approved outfits already hung in the garment bag on my closet door.

We were supposed to spend tomorrow evening doing each other's nails. That agenda had suddenly taken a left turn.

"Slice is coming?" The news buoyed me.

Slice was the model Mom had used several times on the covers of her various books. I met him at a photo shoot she'd arranged for a custom cover. Sparks flew immediately, at least on my end. Since then, we communicated through DMs and the occasional text. Any day I received a message from him was a good one.

I wasn't sure if she realized we'd kept in touch.

She beamed at me. "I was hoping he and your sister would hit it off."

So that was a no. She remained unaware of my close friendship with Slice, and my huge crush on him.

I pursed my lips, the green-eyed monster creeping in. It wasn't like me to get jealous, but then again, my mother rarely meddled in my sister's love life.

"It isn't like you to play matchmaker, Mother," I said with a pissy little sniff, unable to keep my thoughts to myself.

Hands on hips, she squinted at me. "That's enough, Effie Monroe. Get off your frigging high horses. Your sister can't attend and asked you to switch. You agreed. Deal with it."

Clueless about me as usual.

Mom lived in her own little world where bikers, billionaires, and bad boys did anything for the women who loved them. Be it spending extravagant amounts, protecting them from any and every threat, or giving them earth-shattering orgasms, nothing was out of reach if it meant their special ladies were happy.

I wondered what she did with Dad.

Then I tried my best *not* to wonder and refused to let an iota of repulsive speculation enter my brain.

"I'm just surprised you thought to set up Cassie with Slice."

Guilt crossed her face and she walked to me, then sat on the edge of my bed. She glanced over her shoulder. "Your dad doesn't know," she whispered. "Neither does Cass, but I don't like Chad. I think he cheated on her."

Duh.

Chad was always cheating on Cassie. Her life of denial was what made her so irresponsible. She was twenty-five years old and had dated that asshole since she was seventeen. She knew nothing but him and wasn't keen on expanding her horizons.

A month after they met, he hit on me at my thirteenth birthday party. When I told her, she refused to believe me. Until he flipped it and accused me of flirting with his raggedy ass.

In that motherfucker's dreams.

It was then the animosity between Cassie and me began. We'd been quite close once, but she had it in her head that I wanted her man. She ignored his many red flags and placed the blame elsewhere. In that way, she was just as toxic as him, so maybe they were perfect for each other.

A match straight out of hell.

"I don't think Slice is Cassie's type," I blurted. If Mom had a little more awareness about me, my annoyance would've given me away.

Mom waved the words away. "Slice is a model, sweetheart. I think she'd love his glamorous lifestyle."

Like I said, Mom lived in her own world. How was it possible for a woman so reliant on social media for reader and fan engagement to be ignorant of the fact that her favorite model was an actual outlaw biker?

Minutiae overwhelmed her. She rarely handled her socials. It was another task relegated to me. Not that I minded. I was a marketing major with a passion for photography. Helping my mom built *my* portfolio and gave me real world experience.

"Daria!" Dad called from the small hallway that separated the bedrooms. His footsteps pounded against the hardwood floor until he reached my door and walked into my room. "Hi, honey," he said to me.

"Hey, Dad."

Perfunctory greeting out of the way, he gazed at Mom, his hazel eyes practically morphing into hearts.

My parents adored each other. Mom often said she wrote to give the world a taste of real love. They'd been married for three decades, raised three children—my older brother lived in NYC—and were still desperately in love.

I believed that was why Cassie stuck it out with Chad. She thought he'd suddenly turn into our strait-laced businessman father. Never would happen, but she refused to listen to any of us.

Twisting an escaping curl around her finger, Mom stood and casually walked to Dad. She whispered to him, and he chuckled.

Mom turned to me. "Effie, if you really don't want to come, Lennon is happy to serve as my assistant." She indicated Dad with a flourish of her tanned hand.

I laughed nervously, not wanting to tip my hand. What she missed, Dad would home in on and the fallout would affect Slice.

One, I didn't want Slice to lose Mom's gig. Two, I didn't want to miss the opportunity to spend time with him. He'd been my ultimate crush for over a year now, and I desperately wanted to get closer to him. Whether he knew how down bad I was, I couldn't say. Until recently, he'd kept in touch fairly regularly, so that meant something.

Right?

I hadn't heard from him in about a month. I wasn't sure why he'd ghosted me. Mom crossed all her 'Ts' and dotted all her 'Is' whenever she attended a signing, but MMM was like one big family and popular with the readers. No doubt she spoke to him *today* before she told me. Obviously, he had no problem answering her.

I pretended the evidence he'd dropped our friendship didn't chafe.

"Why don't you stay home?" Mom continued into the silence. "It's a bum way to start your spring break. I'm the writer. You aren't. It isn't your responsibility to help me if you had other plans."

Well, shit on a fiddlestick.

"My plans are already canceled, Mom," I said innocently.

My plans could resurrect faster than...nope, wasn't saying it.

"I won't have anything to do if you leave me behind at the 11th hour." Even if she'd invited me at the 11th hour. "Besides, Dad has his fishing trip with Uncle Mike. Remember?"

Mom and Dad exchanged uncertain glances.

"I need the money," I announced. "There are several new outfits I want from *Fashion Nova*."

Disapproval contorted Dad's face. He wasn't the biggest fan of my sartorial choices. Mom, however, totally understood and nodded.

"By the way, Effie, change of plans for tomorrow night," she told me.

Shocked by her words, I snapped my brows together. I wasn't complaining. Unless they involved Slice, her changed plans would make mine easier to facilitate.

"I held a contest and I'm meeting four of my readers for dinner," Mom announced. "You'll be on your own tomorrow evening."

I handled her contests. "But—"

"You've been slammed with your multimedia project for that class." Her mouth turned down.

Mom wanted me to join the writing empire she envisioned and had zero respect for my college career.

"I turned in the project weeks ago," I gritted, my hackles up. I drew a deep breath. "It's fine, Mom. I'm glad Dad helped you."

"Cassie helped me," she said pointedly. "Your father has his own work obligations."

"Awesome." I pasted a smile on my lips. "At least Cassie found something productive to volunteer for rather than sitting around pining over Chad the Cad."

Mom laughed, walked to me, and kissed my forehead as if I were two. "Chad the Cad. Love it, Effie. But she didn't volunteer. I paid her. She wouldn't do it for free."

I would not lose my fucking temper. Wouldn't do it. If that happened, I faced a miserable four days. At least at home, I had the option of locking myself in my room.

"She does have a household to support," Mom added.

"She handed that money over to Chad," I yelled despite myself.

Mom shrugged. "It was hers to do as she sees fit. There's a reason you're our angel and she and your brother are the problems."

"You're our favorite," Dad piped in with zero shame.

They could've kept their favoritism. I wisely kept my mouth shut.

"We were supposed to try out different looks tomorrow evening, Mom," I grouched.

"I'm too grown for that nonsense, Effie." Mom returned to Dad's side. "I'm so disappointed Cassie couldn't come with me. A problem she may be, but she's fun. We would've had a blast with my readers. You're all about the books and your future."

That's all my parents wanted to recognize about me. I ignored the pain of that thought. Once Mom started writing, she characterized her family according to the archetypes she created. I was her Mary Sue. Cassie was the Bad Girl anti-heroine. Heath was the villain. He'd flown the coop, a fact that still upset my parents. And Dad was the ultimate hero.

Ignoring my annoyance, Mom pursed her lips. "I wonder if Slice can join us?"

"Call him and ask him, babe," Dad said. "Throw in an extra five hundred."

"Brilliant idea, Lenny," she cooed and sashayed past Dad.

He watched her walk away and grinned sheepishly at me. "I'll, uh, help Mom try to convince Slice to spend the evening with her and her readers."

Not if I convinced him to spend it with me.

The moment Dad left, I grabbed my phone and shot off a text message.

My mom told me you're attending. Let's meet for drinks tomorrow evening.

SLICE

"Come back as soon as you can, Pretty Boy."

The national president of Red Rum smirked and stared into my eyes as he said 'Pretty Boy.' I held my tongue since I couldn't very well correct the president, unless I wanted my ass beat for disrespect. Besides, I'd had that nickname since I was a tyke. To me, it had never crossed over into *this* life, but Riker never gave a fuck. My twin, Drifter, and our father thought I was shitting them when I announced I wanted to abandon the name. They backed me up, but Riker Reinhardt was the president, not them.

Unfortunately, he declared my road name remained Pretty Boy. I wanted a more badass name. My modeling career was already the subject of jokes, and my moniker didn't do shit to help me. No matter how fucking accurate.

"Did you hear me?" Riker snapped.

Fuck, I hadn't answered.

I quickly amended that and nodded. Didn't want the motherfucker thinking my tongue was useless. More than one chick would counter that point. I fought back a grin at the thought.

Riker's severe look wiped away my smile and sent a chill down my spine. He had salt-and-pepper hair, leathery skin, and mean eyes. When Riker visited, I got my marching orders long before he arrived.

Except my request to attend the book signing as Daria Monroe's model put me directly in Riker's path. I didn't understand how Drifter dealt with him on a day-to-day basis. Thank fuck, I patched in at Dad's chapter instead of hightailing it to Vegas so my twin and I wouldn't be apart.

It was hard in the beginning. Drifter and Dad didn't have the best track record, so I understood why my brother jumped at Riker's offer. But I'd take Dad any day over that psychopath.

Riker looked at Dad. He sat on the other side of the bar, since Riker—as national president and the president of the Mother Chapter—planted himself at the podium. I'd thought the matter of me attending Motorcycles, Mobsters, and Mayhem was settled, since I'd put in my request when Daria first contacted me several months ago.

Before I ended up with a bounty on my goddamn head. But Austin, TX was not Las Vegas or Oklahoma

City, my home chapter and the second largest in Red Rum MC's fifty-chapter organization.

Not one in each state. More like clusters across ten states.

Recently, I was accused of stealing a big drug shipment from one of our biggest rivals.

Stealing was beneath me. It was an *interception*.

Goose—Dad—and Riker congratulated me. Even after the shit hit the fan with the Satan's Sinners MC. I was doing it on their orders anyway. They didn't like my modelling gigs much and wanted me to prove I still belonged in the club, that I hadn't gone 'soft.' They would've been fucking outraged if I shared that I'd once considered modeling full-time again and abandoning the outlaw lifestyle.

"If I hadn't given my permission, your ass would be gearing up to ride out with me, Goose, and Drifter." Riker's tone was just short of chastising. "Lucky you, you accepted that writer bitch before you stole that merch."

Still didn't say shit. The motherfucker was notoriously erratic, but he was all about money. It bought loyalty.

I glanced at my brother. It felt good having my twin with me again. Since he'd left, I didn't see enough of him. Drifter sat next to me, drinking a beer. Riker hadn't shut his goddamn trap since they blazed in an hour ago to scoop up my dad and several of our members to head to Jackson, Mississippi.

For me, it would be a straight shoot down I-35. Dad, Drifter, and the others planned to branch off around the Dallas-Fort Worth Metroplex and take I-20.

"Pretty Boy," Raptor called. He held up one of Daria Monroe's books. One of her bestsellers, which featured me against a blue and black background surrounded by dark smoke.

She'd gotten this idea to pose me like that actor in the centerfold of *Playgirl Magazine* from decades ago. She swore it would catapult her sales through the roof. She was right, and she compensated me well for it.

One of the club chicks loved romance novels. I thought they filled a woman's head with nonsense, but that was just me. I was feeling the chick at the time, so I agreed to take her to the signing.

And chitty bang, chitty bang, bop boo. Next thing I knew I was posing for Daria's covers, immersed in modeling again.

It dawned on me that Riker had finally walked away from the podium. A glance around the room didn't reveal his location. He'd either gone through the bat wings that led to our small kitchen or went to the can.

Dad walked over to me and clapped me on the back. "Be careful, son."

Worry wreathed his features. He had a long neck with a prominent Adam's apple and a long, sharp nose. Hence, Goose.

I glanced from him to Drifter, a reflection of myself right down to the long brown hair, dark eyes, and neat beard. "You sure you don't want to ride with me? Don't want those assholes to mistake you for me."

"By the time you come back, we should have a solution," Drifter swore.

My brows raised. "No shit?"

Dad leaned in. "It isn't guaranteed, but Riker is going to talk to Satan's Sinners' leadership."

"And he's taking Drifter?" I gaped between Dad and Drifter.

"We don't have the same fucking rockers."

Assuming a motherfucker took the goddamn time to read our patches. I'd stolen a quarter rock worth of their drugs and made them look like fucking assholes. A cardinal sin, considering the street value. They'd see only *my face*, shoot, and not give a good fuck they'd fucked up my twin instead of me.

"We have the same goddamn face."

Unconcerned, Drifter shrugged. "I'll be fine."

Asshole sounded as if he didn't give a fuck. Ever since his old lady OD'd, I believed he had a death wish. I scowled at him, because even if he was sick of being among the living, *I* didn't want to bury my brother.

Sliding off the stool, Drifter drained his beer, set the mug on the bar top, and raised his hand. "Save it, Slice."

Other than Daria and sweet little Effie, Dad and Drifter were the only ones who honored my wishes to call me by my preferred road name. Though Oklahoma City was my home chapter where I shared enforcer duties, I was a national special enforcer. I was a crack shot, but I handled knives even better, so Dad and Riker sent me out to slice motherfuckers.

Why *wouldn't* I have that name?

Of course, they dare not call me that around Riker since he shot my request down for his own goddamn amusement. He enjoyed my fucking discomfort.

My phone beeped with an incoming text message. Daria or Lennon I supposed. She was usually a bundle of energy. Now, she was a ball of nerves, concerned I'd disappoint her and thus her readers after I explained I had work-related issues. Didn't bother telling her a bozo was gunning for me. I'm not sure it would've mattered, but I'd opened a can of worms, and they all annoyed the fuck out of me. As Lennon explained, I'd just added to Daria's stress. Two fucking hours ago, I assured her I'd attend, so I couldn't imagine what they wanted now. They'd been calling and texting all fucking day.

I read the message. It took me a moment to realize Effie sent it. Other than an odd video chat here and there, I usually kept in contact with her on the Gram. It was easier. Although she rarely used it nowadays, giving her my cell phone number was a mistake. I suppose she skipped our DMs because I hadn't responded to her in days.

Our messaging had gotten uncomfortably *comfortable.* When I realized how much I looked forward to communicating with her, I pulled back. It also helped that I was laying low and trying to save my fucking ass. Meaning I didn't have time for a pretty girl full of sass and not enough sense to stay away from me.

A hundred-thousand-dollar bounty was no fucking joke. Motherfuckers would hand me over for a quarter the amount.

A moment later, another message came through.

> **Daria: Some of my readers won a contest to dine with me. Please come and make their nights. I'll throw an extra five hundred in as payment.**

Technically, she was my boss, though I preferred to think that we teamed up. But she paid for my lodging, my food, and my transportation, (in this case the cost of fuel for my ride). She was also responsible for my behavior at the events. I *should've* accepted her invitation to the dinner. It was the smart thing to do.

Effie, with her sun-kissed elfin face, her wealth of dark hair, and sweet voice, had fucking trouble written all over her cute little ass.

Sometimes *literally*.

She'd sent me a photo of her in sleep shorts with the word 'trouble' embroidered in hot pink letters on the material covering her backside. Once or twice, I jerked off to that image before coming to my senses and deleting it. My mind flip-flopped between Effie and Daria for several minutes. Soon, I'd be at Daria's beck and call. She'd held the contest without my input; therefore, I didn't have an obligation to fulfill.

That decided me. Effie asked first. Besides, I'd much rather have fun with her.

Because, fuck, who ever said I was smart?

Effie

One doesn't appreciate how far one end of Texas is from the other end until you traverse it. The 28th state of the Union is a behemoth, and driving from Corpus Christi, where I'd lived all my life, to Austin normally took five hours. Thanks to traffic, the drive was longer than expected. My mother insisted we could reach our destination without a single stop, if we fueled up beforehand and packed some snacks. She was right, but when we finally arrived at the hotel, my bladder was screaming for relief, and my legs needed stretching.

Unfortunately, a problem arose with our reservation, which further delayed our check-in. My mother insisted I stay with her because she had it in her head that our room required facial recognition, fingerprint scanning, or both. She swore I'd have to validate my own credentials for access.

A huge banner welcoming the attending authors for Motorcycles, Mobsters, and Mayhem stood near the registration desk. Mom's name was listed as a sponsor and I grinned, so proud of her.

The moment we entered our room—using a regular key card—I zipped toward the bathroom.

"Don't be long, Effie." The words floated to me. "I don't have time for anything but a quick shower and throwing my clothes on."

I slammed the bathroom door shut. Mom and I barely spoke on the drive over. I zoned out and kept music playing through my earbuds. Mom drove. However, we'd be in close proximity for the next several days. Bygones had to be bygones.

As usual.

Once I did my business, the niceness of the hotel room sank in. It was leagues better than the motel rooms normally booked during family trips.

"The bathroom is free now," I announced to my mother when I walked out of the bathroom.

Mom lifted her head and halted rummaging through her suitcase.

Boxes of books and swag filled one hotel cart. Since we arrived two days before the signing, we'd spend tomorrow sorting the preorders, the special swag reserved for readers who placed huge orders, Mom's raffle baskets and the games and prizes for on-the-spot wins at the table.

Flashing a smile, she retrieved her small toiletry bag and the dress I hurriedly added to our garment bag for tomorrow night's dinner. "All right, I'll be out in a jiffy, sweetie."

I nodded, resisting the urge to snicker. What the fuck was a jiffy? After years of hearing her say it, the word had yet to become unamusing.

While my mother locked herself in the bathroom, I plopped down on my bed, opened my IG app on my phone, and notified Slice of my arrival.

Me: I'm here :)

Slice: Sweet

His reply came within minutes. After weeks of slow responses and radio silence, his quickness delighted me.

Slice: Can't wait 2 see u.

Grinning, I bit back a squeal.

Me: The feeling is mutual.

Much to my disappointment, he didn't reply. He didn't even open the text. My smile turned into a pout. Undeterred, I looked at the bathroom door and listened for signs my mother would soon walk out. The sound of running water relieved me. I took a deep breath and inched my oversized shirt up, revealing my lace bralette. It was cute and comfortable, holding up my girls nicely without pinching my skin. I opened my camera app, quickly snapping a few pics. After a moment of deliberation, I bit my lip, chose the best photo, and sent it to Slice.

My rational side wondered if I crossed a boundary. Being so flirty with one of my mom's models wasn't the smartest choice.

Another part of me—the one that ruled—*wasn't* rational, but jealous and eager. Mom wanted to set up Slice with my sister. I refused to let that happen. The knowledge urged me to stake my claim and finally act on my feelings.

Perhaps, I was a bad sister and daughter, but Cassie wouldn't leave Chad, and Mom never forbade me from mingling with her models. Since she wanted to set Cassie and Slice up, she shouldn't have had a problem with *me* and Slice.

The bathroom door opened and my mother stepped out. She looked positively stunning in 3-inch block heels, and her curls gelled into a sleek ponytail. Her basic makeup of eyeliner and red lips turned her into one of her heroines instead of my mom. I'd always been told I favored her. When she didn't look like a bum, I appreciated that compliment.

"I'm about to head out." Mom smoothed down the royal blue wrap dress I insisted she bring. "How do I look?"

"Beautiful, Mom," I replied.

My phone buzzed and my heart leaped. Slice was responding to my photo. It got his attention. All my friends knew how busy I would be so they wouldn't contact me and risk getting on my mom's bad side.

The phone buzzed again and Mom lifted a brow.

"Do you have everything you need?" Somehow, I kept my voice steady and resisted shoving Mom out the door.

Thankfully, her annoyance cleared. "I think," she said, hurrying to her nightstand and grabbing her purse. "If I need you to bring me anything, I'll text you."

I really hope she didn't. Dropping everything to drive to her location would ruin *my* plans for the evening. She wasn't sure if she'd drink, so she was taking an Uber and leaving the SUV with me.

I loved my mother, but I wanted to spend as much time as possible with Slice tonight, not be an assistant. This might be my only shot to win him over.

However, I couldn't tell her that, so I just nodded and said, "Of course, Mom."

She rushed out the door. Finally alone, I gave into the urge and opened Slice's message. His bare chest greeted me and my breath hitched. His abs were the stuff of dreams, and sexy tattoos covered his skin. Words failed me. I hearted the photo and scanned the accompanying message.

Slice: Hope u don't mind me returning the favor 😊

I giggled, my fingers moving as my mind struggled to process the perfection of his body.

Me: Nope, not at all.

I took a moment to fan myself with my hand. An ache settled between my legs as I viewed his photo again. Goddamn, but he was a fine man. Hopefully, I'd get the pleasure of sampling him before the weekend was over. With that thought, I went to my suitcase, looking for the outfit I had brought just for him. If all went well, it'd knock his socks off, allow me entry into his bed, and, ultimately, a shot as his girlfriend.

SLICE

It looked as if I knew exactly how I'd spend my evening. Effie Monroe's tit pic surprised me. Had she been anyone else, I would've sent her a dick pic. *That* would've truly been quid pro quo.

But, nah. I wasn't sure how down she was for a casual fling. No fucking way in hell would I tie myself to that sweet piece. Not exactly innocent but not cut out for my life.

During the drive down, I ignored my anticipation of seeing Effie and tried to figure out my draw to her.

Still, after hours on the road, I lacked understanding of why the fuck I corresponded with her. It started out as being nice to Daria's daughter. Quite sure the woman wouldn't continue to hire me for her covers and the odd appearance at book signings if I'd been a dick to Effie. However, I could've cut ties with her months ago. Yet, I looked forward to our DMs. Even when I fucked one of the club rats, I couldn't wait to see if Effie messaged me.

"Slice!"

At Daria's call, I froze. I'd been in the lobby waiting for Effie and hoping to avoid Daria. My room was on the second floor just like the restaurant I assumed she would meet her fans.

Effie's mom sailed to me and my eyes widened. I didn't remember ever seeing Daria wearing makeup or dressed so nicely. I had to admit, she was easy on the eyes, an older version of her daughter.

If that was what the future held in store for Effie, she should consider herself blessed.

Daria's smile crinkled her eyes. "It's fate, finding you all alone. You must come with me now."

The elevator dinged and Effie stepped into view. I glanced over her mom's shoulder. I didn't have to tell Effie to hide. Her eyes widened and she darted out of view. Probably into the room where all the snacks were sold.

Daria half-turned, saw no one, and focused on me again. "I won't take no for an answer."

"You have to," I told her, not unkindly. "I have plans."

"Please?" she said with a little pout. "My fans will be sooo happy."

"Spending time with their favorite author will make them even happier."

"Are you seeing someone special?"

She attempted to sound casual, but the broad was fishing. My mind raced. As far as I knew, she was happily married. She negotiated her jobs with me in conjunction with Lennon. Terms for my covers and appearances were usually a joint effort between husband and wife.

Fuck. Who knew with chicks? A lot of them wanted a walk on the fucking wild side, and to hell with significant others.

She tapped my shoulder. "Are you?"

I shrugged. "I'm seeing a friend."

She licked her lips. "Male or female?"

"Why?" I asked slowly, more suspicious by the fucking minute.

Fuck my life, but I couldn't be in a situation where Effie just revealed she wanted to fuck me, and her mother decided to shoot her shot.

"I want to introduce you to someone."

It couldn't be Effie. I already knew her.

"Cassie."

"Who the fuck is that?"

"You sound just like Moose," she squealed. She pressed her hand on her forehead. "Oh, swoon. Already in character. So rough and sexy."

Was she fucking hitting on me or playing matchmaker?

Moose was a fucked up biker name. I'd told her that when she ran the idea of her photo shoot for the biker she imagined by me. Obviously, she hadn't listened.

I glared at her. "I'm not wearing antlers or lounging on a moose pelt."

She waved away the words. "We'll work something out."

I didn't like the sound of that, but I let it go. "Who's Cassie?" I asked again.

She dug into her little purse and came out with a piece of paper. "My oldest daughter. She just broke up with her boyfriend. A total loser. Call her. I think you two would be such an adorable couple." She swiped a lock of hair behind her ear. "Even if she won't listen to advice from Lenny and me, you would."

I couldn't imagine what the fuck gave her the impression that I'd jump in line with her dictates. Not setting her straight because time was wasting, I stuffed the phone number in the pocket of my cut. Had to admit, I was curious despite myself. What type of chick was Cassie for her mom to try and set her up with me?

"For a minute, I thought you wanted me to look after Effie." I left it at that. I didn't know how much her mom knew about how often we once communicated.

Tittering, Daria waved her hand. "Effie? She is entirely too sweet for you." She leaned in, not recognizing she'd just offended the fuck out of me. Didn't matter if I agreed. "She's a social butterfly, but not the most experienced. I doubt she's even had sex yet; probably saving herself for someone special. She has such a dazzling future ahead. She wants to open her own marketing agency someday. Become the biggest in Corpus, if not Texas and beyond." Her eyes brightened as if she were relaying something I wanted to hear. "TMI, I know. I just want you to understand why she's off-limits to you, hun."

Instead of blasting her with a string of 'fuck yous,' I nodded.

"As much as I adore you, I don't want my sweet Effie with you." She beamed at me, too much of a damn ditz to recognize the insult of her words. "Now, are you sure I can't convince you to hang out with me? Hubby says I can double the money."

The offer might've tempted me before Effie sent me the tit pic. Now? Especially considering Daria's conversation? Not for any fucking amount would I agree.

"Still a no-go," I said through gritted teeth, reminding myself that this woman was my employer.

Long ago, Effie had mentioned that her mom could be too straightforward and too clueless. A fucked up combination. I'd brushed the text off as venting, putting little stock into the words. Daria hadn't come across that way.

Keyword: *Hadn't*.

Now, I realized Effie had spoken facts.

"Triple the amount of your fee if you come with, Slice."

"Nope."

Daria never understood I didn't do the modeling for the fucking money. I did it because I'd gone through an existential crisis and questioned my life, so I returned to the life I'd known before my mother's death. I'd wondered if I was a regular motherfucker would my ol' ladies have split.

"She must be pretty special for you to pass up that type of money," Daria chirped.

Effie *was* fucking special.

Inside, I cringed at the thought. Outwardly, I clenched my jaw, stoic determination settling into me.

"One last offer—"

"Save it, Daria," I growled. "I'm not interested."

"Aww, that's too bad. How about—" A frown tugged at her painted lips. The chime of her notification saved me. She dug into her handbag, pulled out a phone, and glanced at the screen. "I must run. My Uber is here, so tootles."

Waving her fingers at me, she turned and hurried outside to the valet parking area. I watched her hop into a late-model SUV. Once it drove off, I turned.

Effie peeped around a corner of the archway that separated the lobby from the bank of elevators.

I waved her over. As she walked into view, I clenched my jaw to keep my mouth from falling to the fucking ground. She wore a short red bandage dress. The material revealed glimpses of smooth skin. Toned arms and legs brought dirty images flaring to life and the mounds of her tits watered my mouth.

Sweet Effie, huh?

Indeed.

She stopped inches from me. My eyes were still glued to her perky breasts. Instead of reprimanding my blatant ogling, the little minx spun with dramatic flair and offered me a view of her round ass. She faced me again and smirked.

"You like the fit?" she asked innocently, as if she didn't know that my cock was rock hard.

"I love it," I responded. It crossed my mind to ditch dinner and drag her back to my hotel room. The one her mother and father paid for.

Fuck, that was low. Even for me.

Daria's words echoed through my head, forcing me to show some restraint. If Effie really was a virgin, she at least deserved wining and dining before an old dirty bastard like me tainted her. Giving her a semblance of a proper date was the least I could do.

I cleared my throat, adjusting to conceal my boner, and gave her another once over. "*But*, I'm not sure if it's bike-appropriate, babe. The wind can be a bitch. Not to mention my pipe...pipes...exhaust pipes..."

Her face lit up. My bumbling words didn't register. They seemed to go in one ear and out the other. "You're taking me on your motorcycle? That's, like, so cool."

She giggled, unguarded and carefree. I couldn't help but chuckle. Then, realization struck me and my laughter died. Because, fuck, what if Daria was right? Then again, did it even matter if she was? Effie was grown, and if *she* wanted a walk on the wild side, who was I to refuse her? Now was not the time for a moral dilemma, not when a laundry list of other sins had long ago tainted my soul.

"I am, sweetheart, and I want you to enjoy the ride," I said, mincing my words so I didn't offend her. "So why don't you go change into jeans real quick? I don't mind waiting."

"We don't have to leave the premises," she coaxed.

Oh, yes the fuck we did. With that sultry look and sexy voice, if we *didn't* leave, we wouldn't eat a thing but each other.

"I dressed for you," she admitted.

It took everything in me to bring on my full asshole. "Didn't ask you to, Effie. Now, run upstairs and change."

Immediately, her face fell. I winced, opening my mouth to backtrack and explain my suggestion. Before I could, she huffed out, "Fine," turned on her heels, and stomped back to the elevator.

What a lovely start to my evening.

Effie

When Slice sent me back to the room to change, I blamed my mom, spawning an unwanted analysis of our relationship as I shed the dress I'd been so excited to wear. She had an image of me that couldn't be further from the truth. Cassie was so much of a dumpster fire, that I must look like an angel in comparison, an opinion Mom was keen to share with anyone who'd listen. I was the 'good' kid, even though many of my friends laughed at the suggestion.

Mom started writing seven years ago during my soccer practice. Day after day, she sat in the bleachers, blocked out the world, and penned her story in longhand. Our family wasn't fabulously wealthy, but we were comfortable enough to where Mom took care of home and hearth, while Dad earned the money and then deposited every cent into my mother's bank account.

Although she set Dad up as the quintessential hero, I think she dreamed up men who stood up to her much more than Dad ever could. Daria Monroe steamrolled whoever allowed it.

Dad admired Mom's strength. Mom loved how Dad deferred to her for everything. My mother was an amazingly strong-willed woman with a fantastic imagination and incredible charm when she chose to use it.

Once Mom's books took off, she and my dad remained wrapped up in each other. They rarely noticed anything about me other than my accomplishments. The year I turned fifteen, I not only broke the glass ceiling, I stomped that motherfucker.

Mom and Dad refused to allow me to go to the skating rink for my best friend's birthday party. One, I hadn't posted any teasers that week for her new book. Worse, I left the soccer team and tried out for cheerleading.

For me, their refusal heralded the last straw. I studied their habits and clocked their activities. After two months, I concluded they turned in at ten on the dot without fail. Normally, when they turned off the TV in the den, I'd stand, too, and head to my room. The first two or three times I didn't, Dad gave me a little pushback. Then, they dropped it.

My next determination established they didn't leave their bedroom until six the next morning. Without fail. Ensuite bathrooms were handy little suckers.

Once I confirmed their patterns, I began sneaking out every weekend at 11 PM. Six years in, I had yet to get caught.

Next year, I'd graduate college. Mom and Dad begged me not to move out until then. Dad telling me empty nest syndrome would hinder Mom's creativity killed my intentions to ignore the demand and move out on my own. Heath lived hundreds of miles away; Cassie was miserable and irresponsible. The Mary Sue archetype fell on my shoulders.

Mom and Dad refused rent from me, so I bought groceries with the money I earned from freelance photography. Out of respect for Mom's creativity, I passed on an internship in NYC at Keegan Enterprises. Ryan Keegan headed their marketing division. I'd read an article about her billionaire husband, known as the Savage Suit, and their romance.

My brother greenlit the idea and offered me the spare bedroom in his apartment. Mom scoffed. She wanted me in Corpus, *at home*, because she needed my help.

It wasn't just Slice whom Mom didn't want me to bind myself to romantically. It was *anyone*. My mom would encourage Slice to contact Cass while also warning him away from me.

Sighing, I smoothed my hair down, looked at the mirror hanging on the bathroom door, and exited the room.

My theory lacked proof; I didn't know what they'd discussed in the lobby and refused to ask. If Slice wanted me to know, he would've volunteered that information. But he hadn't. Instead of appreciating that I'd dressed for him, he told me to change into freaking jeans.

The nerve of him!

I almost left him in the stupid lobby, waiting for me. Humiliation coupled with annoyance and a dose of hunger threatened to ruin all my plans. Yet, I returned to him, wearing my jeans and combat boots. I was still stewing, but, when I saw him pacing, his phone to his ear, muscles straining, his long hair queued, I didn't regret my decision. And when he led me to his Harley, I fell a little in love with him. Any lingering anger melted away.

"Let me help you, babe," he said, grabbing my waist and settling me onto his bike.

"Thank you," I breathed, giddy from the brief feel of his hands on me.

After he stuffed my purse and phone in his saddlebag, he mounted up and revved the engine. The roar vibrated the bike, and a thrill shot through me. As he pulled off, I wrapped my arms around his trim waist and leaned my head on his back. Laughter rumbled from him, though I found nothing funny. I didn't know our destination and I didn't care. My hard work finally paying off left me quite happy.

I clung to him tightly, relishing his closeness. The cool air lapped at my face and neck as the cityscape zoomed by. Our surroundings blurred. Being on the back of a bike was an exhilarating freedom I'd never felt before.

I didn't want to pull my body away from Slice's. No, I wanted to be even closer. With nothing between us, especially clothes.

Everything felt out of a dream and strengthened my attraction to Slice. The moment would forever be ingrained in my mind, and I didn't want it to end. In my life, I'd had two boyfriends, one in middle school and one during my senior year of high school. Neither boy compared to the man Slice was.

When we finally glided to a stop, I examined our whereabouts. It wasn't the smartest move, hopping on a motorcycle for an unknown location, but I trusted Slice. His illegal side hustle aside, none of my dealings with him indicated he was a bad man.

"A bar and grill," I noted as I read the sign. My mouth watered at the thought of food filling my belly. Burger grease and sautéed onions scented the air.

One look around told me we were on a shadier side of town and the diner wasn't a five-star eatery. But hey, mom-and-pop shops offered some of the best food around, and I was positive Slice wouldn't intentionally put me in danger.

"Morty's Bar and Grill." He killed the engine, then helped me off the bike. As he led me inside, he wrapped an arm around my waist. Immediately, I cozied up to him. "I come here whenever I pass through Austin. Bomb burgers and some good ass brews."

"Do you visit Austin often?" He relinquished his hold on me to open the door and I smiled in gratitude. "Such a gentleman."

A chuckle met my teasing, quickly followed by a swat to the ass. My eyes widened and my cheeks heated. Despite the photos we'd exchanged earlier, such forwardness took me aback. Not that I was complaining.

"Don't be too sure about that, sweetheart," he replied, leading me to a wooden hostess stand, one arm slung around my shoulders. "Table for two, please."

The pretty blonde manning the station was scrolling on her phone. When Slice cleared his throat, she looked up, tucking the device away. She smiled at him. Pursing my lips. I quickly masked my sour expression with my own grin.

"Of course." She grabbed two menus. "Right this way, please."

The restaurant was more crowded than expected, and the clientele matched the exterior of the building. More than one biker in a cut dined here. A question popped into my head.

"Did you take me to a biker joint?" I asked Slice the moment the hostess left to put in our drink order.

A brow quirked up. "What? No, Effie. It just happens to be near the Austin branch of Red Rum. And to answer your earlier question, I come to Austin a handful of times a year."

"So, you do come here often."

"If you call two to four times a year often, then sure."

"It's more often than I come to Austin, and I live in Texas."

"Touché," he conceded.

Our banter had me in a good mood, enough so that my empty stomach hadn't turned me into a raging bitch. My heart fluttered at his genuine smile. I prayed our night wouldn't end after dinner. I enjoyed his company. Once the signing ended, I didn't know when I'd next see him. Even if we agreed to give a relationship a go.

I didn't believe in long-distance romance. For Slice, I'd make an exception, though almost six hundred miles stood between Corpus Christi and Oklahoma City.

Picking up my menu, I flipped to the burger section, remembering Slice's earlier comment about the bomb burgers. I found myself torn between the 'All American,' which was just a bacon cheeseburger with the fixings, and the more experimental BBQ jalapeno burger. Both had my stomach growling in anticipation.

"Which burger are you getting?"

Slice had been here before, so I'd trust his judgment. I hoped his choice wouldn't offend my tastebuds.

"The 'Eggcellent Burger,'" he said, not even looking at his menu.

My eyes navigated to his selection. It was topped with bacon, a sunny-side-up egg, and sliced avocado.

Meh.

The 'All American' it was.

My decision reached, I set the menu aside.

Seeing my expression, he chuckled. "Not too impressed with the Eggcellent, huh?"

"I'm not a fan of avocado," I admitted. I cringed just thinking about that too soft and green fruit, with a hit-or-miss flavor. Its biggest offense was how quickly it spoiled.

The waitress arrived, setting down the craft-APAs Slice ordered for us. I took a sip, needing the liquid courage to calm down. Slice seemed content to go with the flow, but the lull in conversation skyrocketed my anxiety. What if he found me boring? What if he wasn't into me, but simply felt obligated to entertain his boss's daughter? The nonsensical thoughts were baseless, but they continued populating my mind.

"And for you, ma'am?" the waitress asked, pulling me back in the moment.

I handed her my menu. "The 'All American,' please."

She looked me over, her eyes lingering on my exposed cleavage before she focused on my face.

Was she checking *me* out?

I cleared my throat.

"Coming right up!" the waitress chirped, disappearing and leaving me and Slice alone once again.

"The 'All American' is good," he praised, sipping the beer.

Either he hadn't noticed the waitress's appraisal of me, or I was delusional.

I mimicked him, sampling my brew once more. Beer wasn't my choice of drink, but the one he ordered for us wasn't half bad.

"So, uh, why'd you change your road name?" I blurted, unable to think of something else to jumpstart the conversation. "I've been researching outlaw bikers. I thought once you earned a road name, you're stuck with it for life."

His eyes widened, then narrowed.

Immediately, I wished I hadn't divulged the information, and I nearly face planted.

"I'm just curious, but if you don't want to tell me, that's cool," I added, attempting damage control.

Instead, my words came out in a hurried, jumbled mess.

Smooth.

Real smooth, Effie.

Flirting was easy for me. I'd been doing it since I hit puberty and knew how to butter a guy up. My mother was an expert flirter, especially with my dad. Cass...well, Cassie only excelled if it involved her boyfriend. The point was, I could be a smooth-talker and had examples of how to do it. And yet, Slice had me struggling.

His tension eased and amusement rose in his eyes. "I don't mind telling you *this*, sweetheart," he said gruffly. "Fair warning. The less you know, the better."

Giggling, I rolled my eyes. "Noted, though it isn't as if I'm in any danger, Slice."

He nodded. "I want my brothers to take me more seriously. 'Pretty Boy' is a childhood nickname and doesn't earn me respect. I'm the butt of so many fucking jokes, it isn't even funny. It's time for a change, and Slice is simple."

"That depends on why you chose it," I decided. He'd explained one received road names based on something about themselves—riding skills, personality trait, or a memorable incident. "Knives slice, right? There was also a soda called *Slice*. And, of course, you slice fruit." I liked that option the most.

His dark eyes twinkled. "What do *you* think my reason is?"

"Oh...uh...I haven't given it much thought," I hedged, not wanting to offend him. Over text, I communicated with Slice with reasonable intellect, but in person, I turned into a flustered little girl.

"Little liar," he said, his teasing note removing the sting.

I flushed.

"There's also slice and dice," he said, picking up where I left off. "The term has origins in the cooking world. Before you ask, I'm not a fucking cook. Never have been. Never will be. A motorcycle slice is a cutout of a bike."

"So, which is it?"

He sipped his beer. "I'll leave it up to you to decide. Tell me Sunday morning at breakfast."

It took a moment to remember MMM was hosting a breakfast the day after the signing, so everyone could say goodbye to colleagues and old friends and bond a little more with all their new acquaintances.

Our conversation lulled once more, and we drank our beer in uncomfortable silence. I wasn't sure how to get our date back on track. The boldness that propelled me to send the topless photo had deserted me. I felt so vulnerable. I didn't know if seeing my mother and dodging out of sight set the precedent for the awkwardness between Slice and me. Or if I was still salty that Slice didn't even care why I wore my pretty dress before he sent me upstairs like a child.

Once he accepted my invitation, I'd carefully folded the dress and packed it in with my underwear.

Usually, my forays brought me to parties and other group events. I hardly ever went on *dates*. Despite my rebellion, I was too busy trying not to be like Cassie. I was too busy trying to protect Mom's creativity.

Sometimes, I wondered if that was just a convenient excuse I used. Deep down, I didn't want to end up with a loser like Chad. Nor did I want a man who catered to my every whim and had no thought of his own. Then, guilt would eat me up and I'd curl back into my cocoon.

I didn't want my choices to affect my mother's career. She loved writing. I loved seeing her excitement. On a darker note, I didn't want to give her the power of *I told you*. I told you to listen to me. I told you that you'd fail.

I told you. I told you. I told you.

I fucking *hated* those three words.

Refusing to get into a deep dive with Slice about why my life stood still, I clammed up.

Everything I could've asked, Slice had already covered in our DMs. He wasn't married and had no kids. He was a twin and they, along with their father, belonged to Red Rum MC. His mother died ten years ago when he was seventeen. As a child, he'd modeled for catalogs and magazines. He took it up again after meeting my mother because he wasn't sure he wanted to continue being a biker. Once, he'd dreamed of owning a shop where he built custom motorcycles and refurbished old cars. We talked about visiting all fifty states on the back of his bike. Well, except for Hawaii.

Once we finished our tour of the states, he promised we'd backpack across Europe. All after I graduated.

I promised I'd one day cook all his favorite meals. I'd try to watch NASCAR if he promised to watch football games. We *knew* each other. More than that, I'd believed him. When he ghosted me, I realized he'd just been talking. Or dreaming.

Some dreams weren't meant to be realized. They were just imaginings to propel us to the next phase of our lives. Slice needed Mom's modeling gigs to get through whatever he'd gone through. He seemed to have come out on the other side.

Yet, he was here with me. Maybe, I *could* be a part of his life and he a part of mine. If I knew how to make that happen.

Gazing into his mesmerizing eyes, breathing in his spicy cologne, I wasn't sure what more I could ask him that wouldn't come off as if I was a repetitive dummy.

I deflated. My date was crashing and burning because we had zero chemistry.

"How many dates have you been on, Effie?"

Damn. Slice's question shouldn't have surprised me. If I felt the awkwardness, he did, too. But I refused to go down in the flames of failure. "A fair amount," I said with a straight face.

His grin called me a fucking liar. "I'm still the same Slice, sweetheart. I won't bite," he said gruffly, and winked at me. "Unless you ask me to."

Staring at his mouth, I licked my lips. My pulse sped up and I squirmed, imagining our tongues touching, tangling, and tasting each other. Heat swept through me. Suddenly, I was happy he'd ordered me out of the bandage dress. My hard nipples would've poked through the material.

"I might," I returned, the honest words drawn from weeks of pining for him. Now that I had a chance with him, I couldn't screw it up. The reminder stiffened my resolve. I peeked at him through my lashes. "If you let me bite you back."

His eyes flared in surprise, pleasing me. A slow smile curved his mouth and the twinkle in his eyes changed to a hot gleam filled with promise. He lifted his beer and tipped the neck toward me, then sipped from it, his gaze never leaving my face.

If my stomach hadn't growled, I would've leaned over and stolen a kiss. I grabbed my beer and pressed it against my forehead, glad for the cold condensation. When I didn't feel as flushed, I set the bottle on the table again.

"You don't like beer, do you?"

"Not really," I admitted, seeing no reason to lie since half my beer remained and Slice was almost ready for his second. "I prefer margaritas and pina coladas. White wine. Although," I added at his sudden interest, "I'm a lightweight. I can only have two at most and I can't mix my drinks at all. It makes me so fucking sick."

"You should've told me. The bartenders here make a mean margarita." He turned in the direction of the bar. "I don't see Pam. Hers is the best."

"Let me eat first," I said. "I don't want to get sloshed. If I drink on an empty stomach, that will happen."

"I'd hate for our date to end on such a note."

"Really?" I asked shyly.

He nodded. "I've been looking forward to spending time with you." The moment the words left his mouth, he winced. "Forget I said that."

Never in a million years. Those words took up residence in my head and wouldn't easily move out. No matter what he said.

"Why is the club named Murder?" I blurted, attempting to move away from his admission since he seemed so uncomfortable.

"It isn't named Murder. It's Red Rum."

"A palindrome. Murder spelled backward."

"It isn't. Murder is one word. The club's name is two words."

"Probably deliberate, so stop gaslighting me. If you had it as one word, it would be too obvious."

He scowled. "You go from awkwardness to nosiness. I prefer the former."

"You don't have to insult me because I'm right."

"It wasn't an insult," he said flatly. "It was the truth."

I huffed.

"I don't want to talk about my fucking club. The topic's off-limits."

"Fine," I gritted.

He glanced over his shoulder. "Where the fuck's our food?" he asked crossly.

I thought it was a rhetorical question until someone yelled, "It's coming, Pretty Boy."

I still thought Pretty Boy was more applicable than Slice. He was pretty—okay, *handsome*—while Slice could mean something I didn't want to imagine. I hadn't even meant to ask him the stupid question. He flustered me so much and it turned me into an idiot.

To cover my disappointment, I grabbed my purse from where I'd sat it. "Is it okay if it took pictures?" I pulled out my phone, slid my chair back, and stood. "If I can't do it in here, I'll go outside."

My camera would've been ideal, but I hadn't planned on doing anything else but basking in Slice's presence. Now that that plan was up in flames, some selfies were my last minute backup solution.

Slice drained his beer. "Claude," he called, his commanding voice rising above the din. "Effie wants to take photos. She's good. An amateur photographer, so don't give her any shit."

"You got it, Pretty Boy," the same voice, now identified as Claude, responded.

"Don't wander too far," Slice said and sighed. "Our food should be out soon."

I nodded. "Fine."

SLICE

My assholery hurt Effie. I didn't mean to fucking snap at her, but it was bad enough she knew some of what I actually did for a living. Not all of it. Just that I was a 1%. I left it at that, which was still too much.

Given her mother's romanticized view of my life, I couldn't imagine Effie fully understanding the implications. Most people never figured it out. Fuck, some of our members weren't clued in until it was pointed out.

They were in it to party and fuck. Not bad aspirations, but boring as fuck if that was the fucking sum of your existence. Most members didn't join Red Rum to maim, murder, trade drugs, and pimp chicks.

Our chapter oversaw strip clubs. If the girls whored themselves to clients, Dad took ten percent for the protection he provided. He didn't agree with that and tried to offer enough money for the women to survive *without* selling pussy. He expected honesty, and if he discovered a woman lied about prostitution, he let them go. Johns could be brutal motherfuckers. Yeah, Dad would deal with any man who fucked up one of our broads, but he preferred preemptive measures. If they fucked for pay, one of our boys served as their bodyguard until the deed was done.

Other chapters, like Austin, shied away from the darker aspects of the life.

I could've spoken to Effie gentler, but that wasn't me. Moreover, I was stewing in lust with a painfully hard cock. I was also trying to do the right fucking thing and keep the date away from my bed.

She wanted to fuck me, and I wanted to oblige her. Simple.

But so fucking complicated.

I'd fucked three or four virgins in my life. Virgins were a rare breed nowadays and, yet, they came to the club and offered themselves to me like sacrificial lambs. They understood it was nothing but a fuck.

Effie was different.

Her laughter floated to me, and something tugged at my heart.

Or, maybe, *I* saw her differently. That was why I let her stew in awkward misery. I was doing her a favor. Letting her feel as if we had nothing in common.

Video calls and DMs were different from face-to-face dates. We were in each other's space, inhaling each other's scents, watching each other's every move, and picking up on cues. Conversation between us always came easily. I could've filled in the blank spots until she relaxed and joined in.

The waitress who took our orders set my plate in front of me, then placed Effie's in her spot.

"Another beer, babe," I told her.

She nodded. "Coming up."

"Where's Donnie?" She was my favorite waitress. I'd gotten pussy from her on occasion and took her to the club to party several times. "Or has she switched to a day shift?"

"She quit about a month ago," the chick answered and scampered off.

Two months before I earned my patch, I rode to Austin with my father and met Donnie when we stopped in for burgers and sat in her sections. We'd been fuck buddies ever since. Whenever I rode in, I hit her up.

I scrubbed a hand over my face. Or I had. When I came to town six months ago, I hadn't contacted Donnie. Couldn't bring myself to, wrapped in my friendship with Effie and our DM'ing multiple times a day.

Hopefully, Dad had the scoop on why Donnie quit. Pushing her out of my mind and stealing a French fry, I turned and searched for Effie.

I didn't see her. Panic hit me and I roared to my feet. After all, I still had a target on my back and a one hundred grand bounty on my head. Logically, chances were slim to none they'd hunt me here. They wouldn't expect me to show up in Austin for any reason, but especially for a book signing for romance writers. As a model to boot. More importantly, Riker, Dad, and Drifter were headed to Jackson for mediation. Though Satan's Sinners were bigger, they didn't have chapters in Texas.

Another minute passed with no sign of Effie. I was about to leave our food when I saw her emerge from the short hallway that led to the bathrooms. Even from across the room, she was the prettiest little thing in the place.

I waved her over. She reached me just as the waitress returned with my beer, allowing Effie the chance to snap me snatching the bottle. She followed up with a few snaps of our burgers.

"Anything else?" the waitress asked. She wasn't wearing a name tag and hadn't introduced herself.

I should get her fucking name, but Effie's sweet voice intruded on my intentions.

"I'd like a margarita." Effie reached for her backpack and pulled out her ID, then held it up to the waitress. "In case you need it since you didn't ask before. By the way, if my drink adds too much to the bill, open a new tab."

While I appreciated her modern woman mindset, I still side-eyed Effie. "A margarita won't break the bank, babe."

The waitress winked at her. "It's on the house, love." She turned and sashayed away.

Effie's shock followed by a gulp was so comical, I burst out laughing.

"She has good taste," I said.

Effie looked at me and snapped her mouth shut, then giggled. "Not if she can overlook you. You're hot."

"Keep those compliments coming, babe. They're good for my ego."

"As if you need them." She dipped a fry into ketchup, then stuck it in her mouth. "You know you're the epitome of male beauty."

"You have quite a silver tongue."

Instead of taking that praise and running with it, she lowered her gaze, her shyness returning. The waitress brought Effie's margarita and sat it next to her plate, then dug in the valley of her tits. She laid a slip of paper next to the drink.

"I get off at eleven. Call me if you'd like to go dancing."

The waitress walked away, and Effie stared at the phone number, blinking rapidly, at a loss for words.

It reminded me of Daria's request that I call her other daughter. I picked up my burger and bit into it, then chased it with a gulp of beer.

"Tell me about Cass."

Effie raised her stunning gaze to me. Gold, blue, and green flecked hazel eyes, with a startling amber within their depths. I could lose myself in their beauty.

"Cass? My sister?"

Nodding, I took another big bite of my burger, pleased that she wasn't dainty or shy about eating in front of me.

"Why?" she demanded, once she swallowed, then she scowled. "My mother told you about her."

"She gave me her number. She wants me to call her and ask her out."

Straightening, she set her burger on the plate, folded her arms, and sniffed. "I hope you told her that's impossible."

Jealousy wove through the statement. It was so cute that I hid a smile. "What reason would I give?"

"What do you mean?" she gasped. "How about you live in Oklahoma City and Cass lives in Corpus Christi? Distance dooms relationships."

I was happy to hear her speak those words. It meant she understood we'd only ever be friends with benefits whenever we ran across each other. I was no longer an advocate for relationships. One old lady cheated on me. Another one threatened to shoot me and one of the club girls if she caught us talking again.

Fuck commitment and exclusivity. A woman fucked me up. When I fell, I fell fucking hard, and I liked how clearheaded I'd been once I got through my grief when my relationships ended.

I allowed us to finish most of our food before picking up the conversation again.

"Would Cassie appreciate a call from me?" I asked, pushing my plate aside and tasting my beer.

Effie hadn't touched her margarita yet. She stuffed the last of her fries into her mouth, swiped the napkin across her lips, and threw it aside.

"Cassie doesn't appreciate anything that isn't about Chad, her boyfriend," she snapped, her fire dousing her awkwardness. "He's a fucking asshole, which she refuses to see. He's a cheater, a manipulator, and a grifter." She folded her arms again, her defenses back up. "Is Mom paying you to call her?"

"I'm not a goddamn gigolo, Effie," I barked, offended. "I expected you to have a better opinion of me. If I call her, it's because I want to."

"Right." She snatched her drink, wrapped her lips around the straw, and sucked. Hard.

My cock sprung back to life and my nuts throbbed. Images of her pouty mouth wrapped around Big Boy rose in my head and I forgot Cassie, Daria, and every other woman. I wondered if Effie had ever sucked dick. Generally, I didn't allow a virgin mouth anywhere near him.

She sucked again and a little noise escaped her. I adjusted my cock, dug in my cut, and got my cigarettes and a lighter. Something to calm me and take the edge off.

"God, this is delicious," she groaned, setting her drink aside. Color swept into her cheeks and she grinned. "I better slow down. I don't want to end up sloshed."

"You said two drinks were your limit on a full stomach." She hadn't even had one. Just a few fucking swallows. "I would've suggested wine for you."

"There's a lot of tequila in this drink."

Yeah, a lot of *cheap* tequila. Fuck. I hadn't considered that.

I drew on my cigarette and released the smoke through my mouth and nostrils, then flicked ashes on the floor. Some of Effie's light had dimmed. I wanted to blame the alcohol but I knew it was because I brought up her sister. Low diversionary tactics. Leaning back in my chair, I dug in my pocket for the piece of paper Daria handed me earlier. I dangled it in front of Effie.

"If you don't want me to call her, take it and tear it up."

Relief flooded her face and she snatched it from me, tearing it into minuscule pieces. Even if I had the idea to glue it back together, it would be impossible.

My erection eased, so I stood. I refused to have that waitress return to the table and flirt with Effie again, so I walked to the bar and had Claude ring up my tab. I left that chick a two-dollar tip on a sixty-dollar check. Fuck her. She needed to be taught a lesson.

I returned to the table, where Effie was gathering her belongings. I wondered about the photos she'd taken and regretted not asking for a peek. Hopefully, she'd allow me to see the raw images before she tweaked them. Even the risqué photos she'd sent always had a filter slapped over them.

She lifted her gaze to me.

A sweet tenderness unfurled inside my chest. I gave her a half smile. "Do you still enjoy dancing?"

"Always."

"I…" If I took her to the club…fuck, I'd give her the wrong idea, but until I got the call from Riker, Dad, or Drifter that I was off the hook and the bounty on my life was canceled, I wouldn't be comfortable straying too far from where I was known.

The hotel was the exception.

"We can go to the clubhouse. It isn't far from here."

Her eyes lit up.

"But you must follow my lead, Effie. This isn't one of your mother's novels. This is fucking real."

"I'll follow your lead," she agreed, without asking for details.

"When I tell them you're mine and with me, don't ask questions and don't dispute that."

She got to her feet, gazing at me like I'd hung the fucking moon.

I liked it more than I should have. Once we got back to the hotel, I'd correct her. For now, her vigorous nod and soft, "Okay," sufficed.

She trusted me, even though I wasn't worthy of it.

Effie

Although I'd had only a few sips of the margarita, it buzzed through me. Coupled with Slice and the way my arms wrapped around him on the ride to his clubhouse, my body sang. I'd never been to an MC before. The one time Mom went, she took Dad and some writer friends.

Slice pulled into a spot near the end of a block lined with motorcycles. Even in the darkened night sky, the chrome gleamed, and my breath caught. The scent of oil and exhaust fumes hung in the cool air.

Slice killed the engine and dismounted in a smooth motion. He lit a cigarette, shoved it in the corner of his mouth, then laid his big hands on each side of my waist. His touch burned through my clothes, and I shivered. His hands remained in place until I steadied myself, and then he slid his fingers through my hair. The wind had blown it to hell.

He pulled away too soon. Unintelligible music vibrated from the club, but the brick façade absorbed the exact song.

While he finished his cigarette, I tried to repair my hair, wishing I could see him, but we stood just out of range of the streetlights.

He stepped closer to me. He smelled smoky and spicy.

"Ready, babe?" he asked.

"Yeah," I said, unsure of what awaited me but anxious to find out and trusting Slice.

He clasped my hand and started moving. My heart banged against my chest. Asking about his club's name was the extent of my questions regarding his biker life. Long ago, I'd decided he'd tell me whatever he wanted me to know. My nerves got the best of me. After that gaffe, I never expected he'd invite me to his club.

Beams of light now flooded us, *him*, and I felt as if I was seeing the world around me for the first time. A world filled with Slice. I was five feet six inches and he still towered over me. Muscles rippled from him. He commanded attention and—

We halted a few feet from the door, directly underneath a light shining from the top of the building. He glanced up. Before I followed his line of vision, he turned to me and pulled me closer. He wrapped me in his arms and dipped his head.

I stood on my tiptoes and sank into his arms. He swept his tongue into my mouth, and I groaned. My eyes slid closed and my tongue met his. No kiss I'd experienced compared to Slice's mastery. He devoured my mouth as if he couldn't get enough of me. I slid my hands through his hair, wishing he'd remove the leather tie, not protesting when he gripped my butt and backed me against the building. His fingers tangled in my hair while his other hand slid under my shirt, invaded my bra, and cupped my breast. His lips roamed down my neck. I gasped, throwing my head back for easier access.

He worked my nipple to a hard point. I pushed my boob further into his hand, wanting more. Between my legs felt hot and swollen.

"Fuck, but you're sweet," he growled, thrusting his erection against me. He licked the shell of my ear. "I can't wait to get into your pussy." His breath fanned my skin.

"I can't wait either," I said, desperate to feel him inside me. "We don't have to dance tonight. Tomorrow night, after we're done at the dinner, we can go somewhere."

He snickered. "You like dancing, Effie," he said, brushing his lips along my jawline. "I want to dance with you."

My heart sang. He was sweet, kind, and honorable.

My body count was low. I didn't sleep with the boy I liked in middle school. My high school boyfriend was my first, a relationship that fizzled not long after. A frat boy I went on a couple of dates with during my sophomore year of college was the second and last man I'd slept with. I was eager to make Slice the honored third addition.

"Come on, babe, let's go inside."

We came together for a last kiss before he took my hand again and led me to the door.

My legs felt like mush and my mouth felt swollen and *worshipped*. As he opened the door, he tightened his grip on my hand and guided me in. A Kenny Rogers song blasted from a jukebox. A huge emblem of a skull atop flowers and dice was painted on the wall near the pool table. The place was bigger than it seemed from the outside, but still not as big as I imagined thanks to Mom's books. About a dozen four-seat round tables were scattered around the room, most taken by men in cuts. Most stools at the bar were occupied. For every three men, there was one woman.

We were definitely outnumbered. The song ended and the sudden silence unnerved me, especially as the men turned our way.

"Pretty Boy," someone greeted. "What are you and your woman standing in the door for?"

That opened a floodgate of acknowledgments.

"Why does he think I'm your woman?" I wasn't opposed to the idea, but it was still disarming despite Slice's warning. I'd never met these people.

"Cameras," Slice whispered and pulled me forward before I could question him.

We reached a back table tucked away from view, where a bald man just an inch taller than me stood and slapped Slice's back.

"Striker," Slice murmured with amusement. "Still haven't gotten rid of that fucking name."

"Fuck you, asshole," Striker said with a laugh. "Riker was given that fucking name at birth. He should take a road name and leave me in peace."

"He's your brother, so take it up with him."

"I took it up with Mother when that motherfucker told me to change my road name. She said it was okay, so fuck him. Even if she's not a part of the club, she still gets him in line."

Slice turned to me. "See what I have to put up with, babe? Sheer fucking madness." He nodded to me. "Striker, this is my ol' lady. Effie."

Unsure of the protocol, I held out my hand. "It's a pleasure to meet you."

Striker swept his blue gaze over me, then took my hand and kissed the back of it. "Fuck, I wish he hadn't claimed you. I'd love a turn in your pussy."

My mouth formed an 'O' in surprise. Snickers floated up. Meanwhile, I wasn't sure how to feel.

"She's a civilian, asshole," Slice snapped, placing his hand on the small of my back and guiding me to a seat at Striker's table.

"Must be the night for them," another man called. "Prissy's showing around some author and four of her fans. She took them around the corner to the trailers. That woman thought we lived on the premises. Our chapter's not big enough for that."

"Dorie or Darie. Something," Striker grunted, swigging from his bottle of alcohol. My heart skipped a beat.

My mother had taken her readers to dinner, then came to a *biker club*? Horror washed through me. I couldn't imagine the danger she'd placed herself in. Bad enough. However, if she found us here, I was so fucking cooked.

Striker seemed unaware of my panic. "Prissy's a big fan of hers, especially since you're on several of her covers, Pretty Boy."

"That's right!" someone boomed. "You're lucky Riker only wanted you to intercept that drug shipment instead of icing a few motherfuckers."

"Better you than any of us," Striker said. "I'm just here 'til Riker disbands this chapter. We never got the foothold he promised."

"There might be reasons for that," Slice responded. "Nothing wrong with partying and pussy, but a chapter needs a different sort of presence to move to the top."

In addition to being one of the sexiest and beautiful men I'd ever met, he was a strategist. Sighing, I tilted my head and smiled at him. Thick eyelashes rivaled mine in length, surrounding deep chocolate eyes. I could stare into them for an eternity.

"We try to stay away from murder, Pretty Boy," Striker continued. "That's your specialty."

The words penetrated my dreaminess. My gaze flew to Slice's. He refused to meet my eyes. My heart went out to him and his mortification over that blatant lie, so I reclaimed his hand and squeezed it.

"He's called Pretty Boy not only for his looks," I said. No one else intended to speak up on his behalf. I knew about outlaw bikers. Slice might involve himself in illegal activities, but I couldn't see him committing *murder*. "He has a beautiful soul. He could never *ice* anyone."

Slice stared at me, then his gaze softened, and he leaned closer to brush his lips over mine, ignoring the titters from his brothers. "Thank you, babe."

"You really got her fucking hooked, huh, Slice?" Striker chortled, slapping his knee as if my defense were the funniest joke in the world. "Got her good and dickmatized."

If only.

Instead of responding to his crudity, I focused on the bigger problem: my mother's presence.

"We have to leave," I whispered. "My mom can't find us here. You love working for her. I'll be in trouble but so will you." Any time she wanted to introduce him to Cass, she'd fire him if we were caught.

As for me, the emotional beatdown wasn't worth it.

"You're right." Slice looked at Striker. "Can you call Prissy and ask how much longer before they return to the club?"

Striker shrugged.

"How about you, Desmond?" Slice asked the guy who'd first let the cat out of the bag. He sat at the bar with a line of empty beer bottles in front of him.

"They're on the way back," Desmond answered.

Slice scrubbed a hand over his face. "Fuck."

The novelty of our arrival had worn off. Conversation amongst the bikers and the few women resumed.

"Forget her," Striker ordered. "We need to talk about the trouble you're in with Satan's Sinners."

"Not in front of her," Slice snapped, nodding to me. "Effie's a civilian."

"Don't give a fuck. *You're* here. If those motherfuckers happened upon you, where the fuck would that leave us? Helping to protect you, fucker. Either we go to my fucking office and leave her here or you talk *now*."

Slice shot Striker a putrid look. Neither of them cared about the urgency of the situation with my mom.

"Riker went to Jackson to straighten it out," Slice answered. He made no move to tell Striker we had to leave. "Hopefully, by this time tomorrow, shit will be cleared up." He gave me a hesitant glance and added, "And my bounty will be paid."

Bounty?

I squinted. What bounty and why?

Striker's blue eyes narrowed. "Just be careful, Pretty Boy. As chapter president, I have to make sure my brothers are safe. That includes you, but I don't want you to bring hell to our door then hightail it back to OKC and leave me with the fucking fallout."

"I won't," Slice promised. "It's handled."

That was all I needed to hear. Moving on to the more urgent problem: We needed to leave *now*.

I stood. "We have to go."

Striker glared at Slice. "Handled, huh? You sure about that? Motherfuckers just don't forget what the fuck you did, Pretty Boy."

"Do you know something that I don't, Striker?" Slice demanded, ignoring me.

"We have it on good authority that Dutch is in the vicinity."

"Fuck. Are you sure? I heard he wiped out a few years ago."

"He survived. The Satan's Sinners only bring him out for special assignments."

Slice heaved in a breath. "Any recent photos of that slippery motherfucker?"

Striker found a photo on his phone and slid it to Slice. I was close enough to see the picture. Though average-looking, he stood out from the crowd because of his thick, red beard.

"He looks like an artificially swollen scrotum."

My observation earned a laugh from Slice and Striker.

"Agreed, sweet thing," Striker said as my mother's voice traveled to me.

I froze. Slice froze. Striker cocked a brow.

"Oh my god, where's the music? I leave for an hour and the party dies!" my mother exclaimed, her drunken laughter traveling to me. Thank God I remained in Striker's secluded corner.

My panic deepened and I turned to Striker.

"Where can we hide?" I whisper-yelled, keeping my voice low so Mom didn't hear me.

Throngs of people concealed her from view. The clubhouse may have been small, but it was filled to the brim. However, I didn't want to draw attention in any way, including talking an octave too loud.

Striker snorted. "This ain't a sitcom, girlie; I'm not doing all that shit."

"C'mon, Effie. We can go out through the kitchen," Slice said, grabbing my elbow.

We hadn't taken two steps when Striker called, "Aw, shit, y'all come take a seat. Dolph and Raider, get your asses over here!"

I looked at Slice, but he offered no explanations, a theme for this evening. Instead, he guided me back to Striker's table, slinging an arm around my shoulders once we sat down. Seconds later, two burly men walked over. One of the men—I assumed Dolph—was bald and had a dolphin tattoo on his head. When they eyed me and their gazes lingered on my cleavage, I leaned closer to Slice.

He glanced at me and scowled, glaring at the newcomers. "Watch where the fuck you're looking," he snapped, picking up on my tension and discomfort.

The men shifted their attention to him.

Neither looked happy with his interference, but before either spoke and drew attention our way, Striker whispered, "Dolph, Raider, this is Effie, Slice's ol' lady. Her pussy's off-limit, so leave her be."

"Yes, Prez," the men chorused.

Striker nodded at their obedience, and Slice relaxed. Their leers creeped me out. When they turned away, I felt profound relief. However, my mother and her readers' safety concerned me. If Slice hadn't laid claim to me, I'd be in a pickle. A motorcycle club wasn't the best place for a group of unprotected women.

"Now, I need y'all fuckers to guard my table." Striker leaned back against his chair. "Don't let those book ladies see us, got it?"

The men looked at each other, then back at Striker, their confusion obvious.

Their hesitation pissed their president off, and he barked, "Stop fucking dillydallying and do what I told y'all!"

"Yes, Prez," they repeated, turning their backs to us as they formed human shields.

"Umm, thanks," I said, twisting one of my curls around my fingers. "I'll be in major trouble if she catches us."

Striker shrugged, taking a swig of his beer. "I wanna see how this plays out. That can't happen if y'all leave."

Wow. How generous.

I didn't appreciate being his amusement, but I had the sense not to say anything. Striker ordered one of the club girls to bring drinks to us. Without complaint, I accepted a beer from a half-dressed redhead. Her pierced nipples caught my attention. My face flushed, and I avoided looking at her tits again.

"Thank you," I muttered, swigging the brew and almost gagging.

While the restaurant's beer had been so/so, whatever poison lurking in this bottle tasted like cold piss.

Slice chuckled at my reaction, plucking the bottle from me. "Don't drink it if you don't like it, sweetheart."

A loud moan stopped my reply. Striker motorboating the redhead, who now sat on his lap, grinding against him, horrified me. When he came up for air, he looked at Slice and began a conversation as if a woman wasn't dry humping him. In contrast to my discomfort, Slice looked unfazed by the lewdness. Then again, why would this scene bother him? This was his world, and I'm sure he'd seen worse. Maybe, even participated. The idea twisted my stomach into knots and forced me to confront the reality of his lifestyle.

Needing a distraction, I peered around the men guarding us to locate my mother. I couldn't find her, and I damned myself for losing track of her. That didn't bode well.

The music shifted from country to a 2000s Britney Spears song. *Toxic*, which my mother adored. Even with the noise, her squeal was easy to pick out. Striker was less excited, scowling the moment the iconic song blared through the speakers.

He took a big gulp of his drink and then slid the empty bottle away. "Oh, fuck! Not this shit."

"I love this song," the redhead breathed, no longer grinding against him like a bitch in heat.

"Well, I don't," he growled, setting her aside and getting to his feet. "Okay, turn this shit off, and all visitors get the fuck out! I have a meeting, and I don't want any bullshit distracting me. If you're not affiliated with the club, leave."

I looked at Slice, concerned we were being kicked out. "Should we sneak out the back?"

He shook his head, still lacking the urgency riding me hard. He was so laid back, a quality I found insanely attractive. Growing up around high-strung, dramatic people, gave me the insight to know I didn't want that in a partner. I decided to take a cue from Slice. If he wasn't panicking, why should I? He knew biker protocol better than me and they'd kept my mother away from me thus far.

"Nah, babe, he's not serious. He's just getting her away from us," Slice reassured me. "He doesn't take meetings past sundown. That's 'party time,' as he puts it."

Oh.

It was a ploy.

"Got it," I said, then I processed the second part of his sentence and giggled. "He seriously says that?"

"The man doesn't play about his downtime," he confirmed, grinning at me.

Neither did I. I was a party girl myself, though what I considered mischief and unruly behavior couldn't compare to my current situation.

"Just one more song." My mother's voice floated to me. "I'm having so much fun with Desi and I don't want it to end."

What? For a moment, my world spun out of control. I considered my mother many things—tunnel-visioned, flighty, determined, helicopter parent—but never a cheater.

She burst into *A —You're Adorable*, a song performed by some old dude who had been dead for decades. She loved to sing it to my dad.

One hand flew to my mouth and the other to my chest in a classically overwhelmed and dramatic signal.

Mom giggled again.

I couldn't listen anymore and started to stand. Slice put an arm around my shoulder and held me in place. He pulled me closer. I tipped my head back, on the verge of losing it. His head descended toward mine. My lips parted and—

"Are you insane?" Mom screeched. "I'm married. I wasn't propositioning you!"

"The fuck you weren't," Desmond barked. "Ask anybody here and they'd say you wanted in my bed."

Mom gasped.

Okay, Mom wasn't a cheater. That relieved me to no end. Her ditziness did not. She'd gotten herself into a dangerous situation.

Slice swore under his breath and slid his chair back.

Once Mom saw him, my date was down the drain. I'm sure he'd keep her from seeing me, but she'd demand his time.

"Desmond, sit the fuck down," Striker ordered before Slice stood. "Author woman, get the fuck out of my club and don't come back if you know what's good for you."

Mom belched. "Priscilla invited me."

"Prissy won your stupid contest," Striker said. "You came. You saw. You researched. It's time to go."

"I came. I saw. I conquered," Mom corrected around another burp. "*Veni, vidi, vici.*"

"Come on, Daria," an unfamiliar female voice said. "Striker wants you and the girls to leave. I'll call an Uber."

"We couldn't get rides on the back of a motorcycle?" Mom pressed.

Groaning, I covered my face. Not only because of her persistence, but my date was a total fucking loss. Other than that earth-shattering kiss, Slice and I hadn't connected the way I'd hoped.

"You better get them there in one fucking piece," Striker growled.

Wondering what I missed, I lifted my head and glanced at Slice. He shrugged.

Chairs slid back, a spur or four jingled, and belt chains rattled. The chatter of women—Mom— peppered the air. The door opened and a breeze rushed in. I swallowed, afraid to hope Mom left. In the silence, I heard motorcycles flaring to life and then fading away in the distance.

Striker returned to the table and threw a pack of cigarettes on it. He sat.

"Thanks, brother," Slice said. "I appreciate your help."

"You should. Did this shit for you, Pretty Boy." Striker leered at me. "Don't let my work go to waste."

"She wanted to dance," Slice said evenly.

A half grin curved Striker's mouth. His eyes were pretty. His contemplation was not. "I'm sure."

As much as Striker's words unnerved me, he didn't stop us when Slice took my hand and guided me to the jukebox, filled with CDs. He handed me a twenty and nodded.

"Ladies first."

I didn't hesitate. I inserted the money into the slot and found *Tennessee Whiskey* by Chris Stapleton. It didn't matter that we were the only couple in the small dance space or that we were the center of attention. The feel of his arms around me, the sound of his croon as he sang the words to me, righted all the wrongs of the evening. We were meant to be. *This* was meant to be.

This was the first day of the rest of my life as Slice's ol' lady.

SLICE

The evening didn't unfold as I'd expected. Daria warning me away from her daughter dashed the few plans I had and completely threw me off. Just when Effie and I were getting back on track, the damn woman popped up again. As Effie's mother and my boss, I'd never openly disrespect her. But she was a bimbo, plain and simple, who put herself and her readers at risk to indulge in a fantasy.

How in the world do you write about fucking bikers for a living, and be shocked when they expect you to pitch pussy?

Women who came to the club were either ol' ladies, club girls who fucked everything in sight, or on the hunt for a biker to rock their world. Those three basic categories were not hard to grasp. Yet, the MC author seemed clueless that she fit the mold for the third category.

And I almost blew my cover, thanks to fucking Desmond, the prick.

Shaking my head, I finished taking a leak, shaking my cock off before I tucked him back in my jeans. Effie had run to the little girl's room, and I'd seized the opportunity to relieve my expanded bladder. Once I washed and dried my hands, I walked out. I'd instructed Effie to head straight to Striker's table if she finished before me. She'd listened, sitting pretty, a vision despite her evident discomfort. Only Striker sat with her, and though he wasn't as bad as some of my club brothers, he was a dirty dog unsuited for the company of someone like Effie.

Strolling over, I held my hand out to her. "A few more songs, then we'll head out."

At the relief sweeping over her face, I side-eyed the fuck out of Striker. He just shrugged and grinned. Instead of pushing the issue, I grasped her hand and tugged her back to the dance floor. *Smile* by Florida Georgia Line was playing, and we quickly found a rhythm, swaying to the beat together.

"What was Striker telling you?"

"Nothing," she replied, a complete load of bullshit.

Her dismissive tone and evasive answer only fueled my curiosity. Chances were a less-than-subtle pass by Striker disgusted Effie. If I got confirmation of my theory, it'd do nothing but piss me off. He outranked me, so beating his ass for disrespecting my girl simply wasn't an option.

Wait.

My girl?

Where the fuck did that come from?

Effie would just be a fling. Nothing permanent or serious. I liked her more than I should've, but the reality of my world dictated a night of fucking would be the extent of our relationship.

Maybe, two nights. We lived almost nine hours apart in our regular lives. No fucking way would I travel six hundred goddamn miles *just* for pussy when I had more than enough available at the clubhouse every day.

"Penny for your thoughts?" Effie's sweet voice seeped into my brooding.

"My thoughts are worth more than a penny, babe," I replied. Her giggle delighted me.

Smile faded into *Fancy Like* by Walker Hayes. We adjusted our groove to match the new song. We didn't say much as we danced, just basking in each other's company.

"Slice?" Effie whispered when the song ended.

A pretty flush colored her cheeks. Fuck me, but she was a beauty.

"Yeah, sweetheart?" My husky voice betrayed my desire.

"Are you going to kiss me again?"

Big Boy sprang to life at her breathy question. Our kiss outside rocked my fucking world. I'd merely meant Striker to see her in my arms, so my claim would be clear and no bullshit would arise. I hadn't expected the depth of her passion or the feeling it stirred inside me. "Do you want me to?"

She was silent for some seconds. Then, she stood on her tiptoes and kissed me. For a moment, her boldness shocked me. Not sure why. This was *Effie*. She took life by the handlebars and went after what she wanted. She nipped my lower lip and I groaned, wrapping my arms around her waist. My brothers' catcalls and hoots broke us apart. The attention turned Effie's brashness into bashfulness. Her cheeks were thoroughly pink.

I caressed her lower lip, swollen from our kiss. "Let's ride out, babe."

She nodded, clutching my hand as I led her out of the clubhouse. The chilly night air greeted us, but didn't cool my blood.

"Where are we going?"

"The hotel," I answered, helping her onto my bike.

Disappointment swept over her features. "Oh."

My hands lingered on her waist. I was painfully hard, and Effie was a grown woman. If she wanted to fuck me, who was I to throw a wrench in her plans?

"You misunderstand me. You won't be going to your room when we get there. You're coming to mine."

It was almost comical how her face lit up, all because the big bad biker would finally give her a taste of what she'd been chasing. I couldn't hold in my chuckle. Leaning down, I brushed my lips over hers, then hopped on my bike and started it up. Typically, I enjoyed nothing more than riding my motorcycle, but tonight, I couldn't get to our destination soon enough.

As we rode in the elevator to my floor, Effie texted her mother some bullshit about meeting up with a friend who'd left Corpus to attend college in Austin. In reality, she was following me to my room for dick.

When the elevator door opened to my floor, I grabbed her hand and practically dragged her down the hall to my room. Her giggle at my eagerness brought a smile to my face.

Inside the room, I kicked the door shut and flipped on a light, then settled my hands on her waist. I took a moment to admire her beauty, my gaze flickering across her face. Filled with lust and excitement, her hazel eyes locked with mine. Her dark curls framed her heart-shaped face, and her lips— *God, those fucking lips*—were parted ever so slightly. Her tongue darted out to wet them and my stomach tightened.

"You're so gorgeous, sweetheart," I murmured, thumbing her bottom lip.

"I can say the same about you." She wrapped her arms around my neck. "But we're not here to compliment each other, so—"

I didn't let her finish her cheeky comment. Her gasp was lost as our lips met, my hands exploring the lithe curves of her body. A thrill shot through me. The warmth of her lips was intoxicating, and the taste was divine, like a sweet summer berry. She melted into me. Her fingers dug into the fabric of my shirt as she pressed closer, the softness of her body a stark contrast to the hard lines of my muscles. Her intoxicating perfume, a mix of vanilla and something musky, filled my nostrils. Our mutual need was a raging inferno, consuming and intoxicating. My tongue slid against hers and her moan vibrated through me.

"Slice," she breathed against my lips, her voice shaking with need. "Please..."

"Please what?" I whispered, pulling back just enough to look into her eyes.

My blood burned at what I saw in those hazel depths.

Desire that rivaled mine. Trust I didn't deserve. And submission she was eager to offer.

"You know what I want," she said.

I swallowed at her boldness. A second ticked by before I found my voice.

"Strip for me," I ordered, stepping away to give her space to carry out my command.

A playful smile touched Effie's lips as she raised an eyebrow. "You want me to do a striptease?"

"I sure do, babe." My dick jerked at the thought of her beautiful skin bared to me. "I want to see every inch of you."

Her eyes widened, but she nodded. "As you wish."

She grabbed the hem of her black cotton T-shirt, pulling it over her head and revealing a black lacy bra that created mouthwatering cleavage. My gaze glued to her heaving tits, my cock threatening to explode in my jeans if he didn't get some relief. She allowed me a moment to admire her before she reached for the button of her jeans. Her fingers trembled slightly and a flush spread down her chest as she slowly slid the denim down her legs. Her eyes held mine. She revealed a matching thong. I groaned. Her jeans pooled around her ankles.

A fierce blush stained her cheeks. She stood before me, completely vulnerable, completely *mine* for the night.

"You like what you see?" she asked, a teasing lilt masking the uncertainty on her face.

"I love what I see." I clasped her waist. "You're absolutely breathtaking."

She clicked her tongue and I paused. My brows furrowed at her slumping shoulders.

"Shit," she mumbled, wobbling back. Away from me. What the fuck? "My shoes."

My gaze dropped to her combat boots. Fuck me. Earlier, I'd ordered her to ditch the heels. More practical for riding, but harder to come off, and impossible for her to just step out of her skinny jeans with them on.

"Turn your back," she said, reaching down to unlace the boots.

Smirking in amusement, I stayed in place.

She scowled. "Now."

"As you wish, Your Highness," I teased and turned to give her the privacy she wanted. I didn't point out I intended to not only see and feel every inch of her, but taste, too.

Fabric rustled. To prevent further delay, I stripped myself, unconcerned about a striptease or looking sexy. My clothes were piled on the floor within a minute. Big Boy slapped my navel as he sprang free, the tip an angry red, a testament to how much I wanted the little minx behind me. Silence urged me to turn. Effie's boots and jeans lay on top of her discarded shirt.

Her gaze flew to my cock. "Oh," she squeaked.

Daria exposing Effie's virginity came back to me. Perhaps, her shock stemmed from me truly being her first, though I couldn't imagine Effie announcing to her mom that she'd fucked. Maybe, I was simply her biggest. Thankfully, she was candid in her flustered state, giving me the answer I sought.

"You're, umm, super big. Like, pornstar big," she babbled, her body a pretty pink. "Not that I thought you were small, but the other guys I slept with were much smaller. Not that I've been with a lot of guys, only two, but—"

"Effie," I interrupted, not interested in hearing about her past exploits.

"Sorry."

I had no right to be jealous of those other motherfuckers, but dammit if I wasn't. However, I felt *some* relief that her mother had been wrong. Effie's experience made things easier because I didn't have to teach her everything.

We were veering wildly off track. My impatience to feel her wrapped around my cock grew to desperation.

She cleared her throat and fidgeted. "I'm fucking things up, aren't I?"

"You aren't, sweetheart," I reassured her gruffly, placing my hands on her hips and pulling her closer. Touching her any place else might spook her.

Hmmm, what had she done with those other yahoos?

"I really care about you, Slice," she said softly, her sweet words touching me. "And that's making me nervous."

I brushed my lips over hers. "Just calm down and let me take care of you."

"M'kay," she murmured, allowing me to guide her to the bed.

She sat on the edge and scooted back, resting against the pillows. Her sun-kissed skin contrasted against the white sheets and her hair cascaded around her shoulders. She was a vision. The moonlight streamed through the window, casting an ethereal glow over her. My cock twitched, a bead of precum escaping.

I joined her on the bed and stretched out behind her. Skimming my lips over her sweet-smelling skin, I moved my hands to her bra and unhooked it with practiced ease. I tossed it aside, leaving her perfect tits bare. My thumb brushed over one of her nipples. She gasped at that small touch. I urged her into the crook of my arms. Her perfect tits bared to my hungry gaze made my mouth water.

Not giving her a chance to dwell on her unclothed body, I brushed my thumb over one of her nipples and her back arched.

"So sensitive," I murmured, trailing my lips down her neck. "I'm going to savor every part of you, Effie."

To prove my point, I wrapped my lips around one of her taut nipples, suckling the pink bud, encouraged by her moans. I swirled my tongue around her tit, while my finger teased the other, rolling and pinching the nipple gently. When I switched my mouth to lavish her other breast with the same attention, I slid my hand to her thong, brushing against the damp fabric covering her slit.

"Sopping for me already," I growled, dark with need. "How long have you been thinking about my cock in you, baby?"

"Every night," she admitted, barely above a whisper. Short, shallow gasps escaped her.

I smirked and tore away the scrap of material covering her pussy. She was so fucking wet. A grunt of approval, a deep sound of satisfaction, escaped me. I teased her clit with slow, deliberate circles, and a low hum vibrated in her throat, a sound both pleasing and anticipatory. I slid two fingers inside her slick passage. With a gasp, she moved her hips against my hand, and her fingers tightened on my shoulders.

"You like that?" I whispered, pressing a kiss to her sternum.

"Yes," she breathed, her body trembling. "Don't stop."

"Don't plan on it."

I curled my fingers upwards, seeking the special spot that'd make her see stars. The tension in her body, the clenching of her cunt, and the quiet expletive she uttered confirmed that I had located it.

"Oh my gosh," she whimpered, grinding against my hand. "I need...I want...fuck!"

At the addition of my third finger, she lost her train of thought, but fingering alone wasn't enough for her greedy pussy.

"Tell me what you want, Effie," I demanded.

"You," she breathed. "I want you."

My ego and dick swelled in unison. I trailed kisses down her stomach and withdrew my fingers. When I reached her lower belly, Effie's legs parted willingly. I settled between them, admiring the pink, swollen lips of her pussy, the wetness seeping out evidence of her desire. I blew gently, teasing her tender flesh. She shivered and I chuckled. My head spun at her feminine scent, so sweet and delicate. Leaning forward, I softly kissed her inner thigh. My stubble brushed against her sensitive skin as I worked my way upward. At the apex of her thighs, I plunged my tongue into her core.

"Fuck!" she gasped, thrashing against my face, her fists clenching the sheets.

The heady flavor of her slick heat hit my taste buds. Groaning, I gripped her hips to settle her and savor her sweet nectar. I used my fingers to spread her pussy lips, exposing her even more to my lapping tongue and allowing me to explore every crevice of her pussy. I switched focus to her clit, swirling the tip of my tongue around it before sucking it between my lips.

"Oh god, yes!" she cried, her slim fingers twisting in my hair, her moans filling the room.

I kept my gaze trained on her face, admiring her blissful expression and heaving tits. Her eyes were closed as she writhed against my mouth, seeking more friction. She trembled and her body tensed. I knew she would soon come.

"I'm close... so close," she panted, her breath coming in short, ragged gasps. "Don't stop, Slice, please!"

Well, who was I to deny such an impassioned plea?

Plunging two fingers into her wetness, I thrusted them in rhythm with my tongue. Effie's toned thighs clamped around my head, trapping me against her heat. With a final cry, she came hard, her juices flooding my mouth as her body trembled. I moaned at the burst of flavor, and I continued to lap at her, helping her ride out her orgasm until she went limp.

On the verge of coming before I sank into her pussy, I couldn't wait another moment. While she was still catching her breath, I pushed her knees to her chest and plunged inside of her. Our voices joined in a single cry, my sudden intensity of emotion making my chest ache and threatening to overwhelm me.

"Fuck, Slice."

Ignoring the sting of her nails digging into my shoulders, I held her legs in place and filled her to the brim. When I bottomed out, I took a moment to adjust to the bone deep pleasure of finally having her in my arms. Soft and vulnerable around me, she gave herself freely, not hiding or holding back. I almost came then and there. I was no one pump chump, but Effie challenged my near-perfect record.

Tenderly, I scrubbed strands of damp hair off her flushed face and brushed my lips over hers.

"You feel so good," I groaned. Gripping her hips, I began moving slowly. "So fucking tight."

Controlling my burning desire allowed me to set a steady pace. Each deliberate thrust was designed to drive her wild. Her moans mingled with mine. Her pussy clenched around me and my eyes almost fucking crossed. My cock dragged along her walls and she responded to each small movement, our bodies attuned.

Short, shallow breaths escaped her. Pleasure glazed her eyes. Her nails repeatedly raked over my back, the slight sting fueling my increasingly frenzied thrusts. Her head lolled to the side. Gripping her chin, I forced her to keep her gaze trained on me.

"Look at me," I commanded, low and rough. "I want to see those beautiful eyes when I make you come again."

She nodded, whimpering a tiny, "Okay." The sound of her sweet voice tightened my balls.

Her eyes sparkled with lust. As she adjusted to the pace I set, she moved with me. Our bodies synced in a primal flow. She fit against me oh so nicely, and if I was more of a sap, I might say she had been designed just for me.

"God, Effie," I breathed, picking up the pace and pushing harder, deeper, into her.

The occupant in the room next door probably cursed my entire fucking lineage, but I couldn't care less. As tension built inside me, my entire world narrowed down to the delicious friction of our bodies.

"More!" Her single word spurred me into a frenzy.

Reveling in the way she surrounded me, I couldn't deny her demand even if I'd wanted to. I released my hold on her legs to grip her hips. My fingers dug into her flesh. She wrapped her legs around my waist, desperately trying to keep up with my vigorous speed. Skin slapping against skin filled the air, punctuated by our mutual cries of ecstasy. Fire coursed through my veins and down my spine.

"I'm going to come again!" she cried, her hold on me tightening.

"Come for me, Effie," I ordered, my voice thick with desire. "I want to feel you come around me. Let go, baby."

With one last whimper, she complied; the tension in her body released as she screamed in ecstasy, a sound that vibrated through her very being. Her slick, hot walls clamped down on my cock. I couldn't hold back any longer.

"Fuck!" I roared, lost in sensation.

A last thrust and I exploded, coming hard and spilling inside her. My vision whited out for a moment and my body shook. When my orgasm subsided, I stilled and collapsed against her.

Catching my breath, I flipped our positions and wrapped my arms around her. She rested her head against my chest, the scent of sex and *her* filling my nostrils. It was a combination I could become addicted to. I could wake up to the comforting warmth of her skin pressed against mine and fall asleep to it every night.

"That was incredible," she murmured, hoarse. Her fingers traced mindless patterns on my pec, the light touch sending electricity down my spine. "The best I ever had."

I chuckled, my chest puffing out in pride. "Same."

She hummed in response; my simple statement seemed to have pleased her. A comfortable silence settled between us, the lingering warmth of our lovema— nope, we weren't in love—of our *fucking*, leaving us both sated and deeply satisfied.

SLICE

Twenty minutes later, we were still intertwined. Though conversation was minimal, my satisfaction ran high. The subtle scent of arousal and her delicate perfume hung in the air. I wanted her again, yet I was loathe to intrude upon our peace.

"So, does this make us a couple now?" Effie's sweet, breathless voice interrupted the stillness of the room.

I tensed and my contentment shattered. She stirred in my arms and tipped her head back. Hope gleamed in her gorgeous eyes. I averted my gaze. A dozen replies raced through my mind. None would be what she wanted to hear. I liked Effie more than I should, but a relationship between us *was not feasible*.

I wanted her, truly, but we could *never* be a couple.

There were logistical factors to consider, like the fact that we lived in two different cities, two different states, and existed on two different sides of the law. Then there was the age difference, her mother's disapproval, and most of all, the danger. While there was a bounty on my head, she wouldn't be safe. Even once that target was removed, I lived a dangerous life. I cared about Effie too much to risk her.

She waved a hand in front of my face, pulling out of my arms to rest on her elbows. "Hello? Earth to Slice."

I focused on her again. Perhaps, she saw something in my eyes. The denial on my face. She was very smart. It was one of the things I loved about her. Whatever the case, her hopeful gleam dulled, replaced by betrayal unbearable to see. Even before I spoke, she knew my answer. Her vulnerability wouldn't sway me.

But she was stubborn, too. She swallowed. "Slice?" Her eyes were huge, her defenses completely down. Her lips trembled. "This was more than a one-night stand, wasn't it?"

I couldn't bring myself to give a direct response. "You already know the answer." She exited the bed and I scrubbed a hand over my face. "Effie—"

"Save it," she snapped. Her voice wavered and I felt like the biggest prick alive. "You just wanted to have s-sex with me! Now it's happened and you're done with me."

She stomped around the room, collecting her clothing.

"Sweetheart—"

"I am so fucking dumb! I can't believe I thought you actually liked me."

"I do like you, Effie." At the admission, I blew out a breath. I didn't want to give her false hope even as I fought the urge to get up and pull her back into my arms. Swear to her I'd love her forever. Fuck, *want* her forever. "I just want casual flings. I don't do anything serious."

"You could've said that before you fucked me!" she yelled, angrily swiping at her eyes.

Her tears almost broke me; a goddamn headache formed. I rubbed my temples. "I didn't think I'd have to state the fucking obvious. You and I have been friends for over a year. I've never once mentioned I had a woman or wanted a woman."

For several seconds, her sniffles were the only sound in the room as she tugged on her clothes. "Whatever," she finally muttered, gathering the rest of her belongings and storming out of the room.

The slamming door rang out like a gunshot.

Guilt rushed through me. "Fuck."

In a romance story, I'd race after her, breathlessly whispering my undying love, vowing that no force on earth could separate us, as the sun set and painted the sky with vibrant hues. Yet, life didn't work that way. *Life* wasn't cheesy, flowery bullshit that chicks loved. Someday, Effie would recognize that my actions, though seemingly harsh *now*, saved her from my fucked-up world.

First, we needed to get through the signing, when we'd be forced to play nice and be around each other all day.

How fucking lovely.

Effie

I had never been a romantic. My parents were wildly in love, but they were the exception to the rule. Cassie, Heath, and my friends' toxic relationships were the norm. Seeing them—especially Cassie and Chad—stopped me from believing in the power of love and all that jazz. Mom and Dad sometimes gave me hope, then I'd think of my sister and her man and remind myself that Mom lucked out when she found Dad. Their love and devotion was pure and unfettered, born from genuine respect and friendship.

Mom wrote her romances based on her relationship with my father. Finding a man like Lennon Monroe who would put me on a pedestal and place me above everyone and everything would never happen. It was straight out of a fairytale—she had the wedding pictures to show the white carriage that carried her to the church and then her and Dad to their reception. She'd looked like a princess and he her knight-in-shining armor. The knight he was and had always been.

I felt so stupid. In the aftermath of my night with Slice, I realized I'd fantasized about him as not only my lover, but my prince in a cut. The man of my dreams who'd sweep me off my feet and spend the rest of his life devoted to me. He'd appreciate my devotion to him, just as Dad adored Mom's.

Slice's rejection doused my dreams in cold reality and reminded me that I didn't really believe in true love. I was just lost in the moment. Now that clarity had returned, I remembered my actual outlook. Deep respect, not love, bloomed with someone you cared about. Or learned to care about.

I believed *Slice* had grown to care about *me* in the same way, but I was wrong.

Our relationship wouldn't have been sunshine and roses, but I thought he'd give me a shot. Nothing good came easy, and couples in lasting relationships put work in. Foolishly, I believed my feelings were mutual. It crushed me at how wrong I was. I was just an easy piece of ass to him, a college girl with a raging crush and nothing more than another notch on his belt.

I was such a fucking idiot.

An angry tear leaked from my eye, and I swiped it away. Unfortunately, more quickly followed. My sniffles rang out through the elevator. I was so thankful I was alone to compose myself before I reached the hotel room. No way I could explain my emotional state to my mother; I simply didn't have the energy.

Thankfully, when I entered the room, she was nowhere to be found. Relieved, I quickly removed my clothes and shoved them back into the suitcase. Once I was in the buff, I trudged to the bathroom, to wash off the sweat and the stench of sex—of Slice—clinging to me.

In the shower, I cried freely. My tears mixed with the hot water raining down on me. I didn't regret sex with Slice; it was the best I ever had, and I doubted anyone would ever measure up to him or his bedroom skills. Yet, I beat myself over thinking he, a bad-boy biker who modeled on the side, would settle for *me*. He likely had a wealth of options. It wouldn't surprise me if the game he played with me, he used on many other women. Get their contact info, befriend them, and then charm them into bed.

"Stupid!" Angrily, I scrubbed my skin.

I wasn't a *romantic*, but I'd fallen hard for Slice. Not love. Maybe. Hopefully. But *like*. Definitely, I'd fallen in like. Though I didn't read my mother's books, I couldn't help but fancy myself his heroine, a regular girl claimed by an outlaw biker who'd give her the world. Instead, he gave me a night of passion I'd never forget and promptly ended things.

"Fucking idiot," I hissed, the insult directed at him *and* myself.

As naïve as I was for thinking that Slice and I could have more between us, never once had he told me he *wasn't* looking for something serious. Stomping on the heart of your boss's daughter certainly wasn't the smartest move. If I was more vindictive, I might open up to my mother, just to fuck things up for him. While I was no angel, I wasn't a raging bitch either. I wouldn't mess with his career just because he screwed over my emotions.

No, I'd play nice at the dinner tomorrow night, and the signing the day after. At both events, I'd pretend nothing happened. I'd look through him as if he didn't exist. I'd wear my red bandage dress he hadn't appreciated and flirt the entire evening with as many hot guys as possible!

Fuck him!

Misery pooled inside me.

Only when my tears stopped did I exit the shower. I dried my body and hair, then wrapped the towel around myself and returned to the room. Getting my toiletry bag, I pulled out my leave-in spray and an oil mixture of rosemary, coconut, and argan oil. My curls loved it. Once I slathered every strand in the stuff, I started to French braid my hair. Halfway done with the first one was when my mother stumbled in, loudly humming a melody I didn't recognize. She escalated to singing. My mother was many things, but an excellent singer wasn't one of them.

"Mom?"

The singing ceased, much to the delight of my ears.

"Effie, darling?" she slurred, breaking into a smile when she spotted me on my bed. "I didn't wake you up, did I?"

I finished the first braid and gathered the rest of my hair to start the second. "No, Mom, you didn't."

"Good."

With my comfort settled in her mind, she began prattling about her night, unaware I'd witnessed part of it, including how careless she turned because of alcohol and the danger she could've been in. I wondered if she'd bring up her trip to the MC.

"...But after dinner, my readers and I weren't ready to end the night, so we ordered a few rounds of drinks," she shared as she removed her jewelry.

Done with my hair, I began fidgeting. "What'd you get?"

Probably something fruity. She loved tropical drinks and spawned my love for sweeter alcohol. Once I turned eighteen, she allowed me to drink at home, if it was a mixed drink, and I limited myself to three. Her imposed rule morphed into my permanent preference, and I liked her drinks far more than the cheap beer I'd drank at high school parties.

Not that she knew I touched a drop of liquor outside of our home before I was a legal adult.

"Sangria," she answered. "Oh my gosh, sweetheart, it was so good. We must go there before we leave Austin so you can try it yourself."

"That sounds great," I replied halfheartedly.

I wanted to show more interest in her night, but my mind kept drifting to Slice. So, I just nodded along and offered small, noncommittal responses. That was until she got to her foray at the Austin chapter of Red Rum MC.

"Oh, and get this, Effie, I went to an actual MC!" she squealed, bouncing on her heels like a toddler as she continued her drunken rambling. "A real biker girl is a fan of my books. Can you believe that? Anyway, she gave us a tour of the MC, and I talked to a flesh and blood biker. He thought I was flirting with him, but the president—such a kind man—smoothed things over."

I nearly snorted. Kind wasn't how I'd describe Striker. Discomfort still lingered at his crude comments while I'd waited for Slice to return from the bathroom. I'd be content to never see Striker again.

In one way, I was glad my mother went out and socialized. At home, she locked herself in her home office and neglected to take time for herself. She rarely saw friends. Yet, I couldn't escape the dread I felt at the thought of how tragic her night could've become, had Striker been more of a dickhead or Slice and I hadn't been at the club. Slice might've been a douchebag, but he certainly would've stepped in to defend her, even if the president hadn't.

"Mom, you have to be careful," I said gently, twirling the end of my braid around my finger. "I mean, it's great that you're having fun, but that could've ended really badly."

She waved a dismissive hand. "I'm a grown woman, Effie. I can handle myself."

Doubtful, but I bit my lip to hold back from saying more. My mother had a way with the written word, but she was a little...*unaware*...when it came to the real world.

Humoring her, I plastered on a smile. "I know, Mom. I just want you to stay safe."

"Oh, sweetheart, I'll be fine," she reassured me, sitting on the edge of my bed and reaching over to pat my hand. "You're so much like your father, always looking out for everyone. But just focus on enjoying your time here."

"Yeah." My smile faltered. "Enjoying my time."

My mother always booked an additional day after the signing to recuperate and explore before we returned home. Normally, I looked forward to that one vacay day. But this time, I just wanted to get back to Corpus Christi and wallow in self-pity until my sadness went away.

To the surprise of no one, she didn't catch the misery in my voice. She was still too caught up in recounting her night. Her lack of focus on me was a blessing and a curse. I could've used a little motherly love. However, I'd also have to scramble to come up with a cover story.

"Help me unzip my dress?" she asked once she'd filled me in on every detail.

I nodded, and she scooted back. The conversation seemed finished, yet, while I was sliding her zipper down, she started to prattle about her run-in with the last person I wanted to hear about. It was hard not to groan in annoyance. My beautiful, bubbly mother was a chatterbox who held nothing back, but tonight, I wish she'd left me in the dark.

"Oh, and I gave Cassie's number to Slice just before the Uber arrived. I hope he called her; she needs a good man in her life."

A good man?

Hah.

The mention of his name was like a knife digging into me, and the last comment twisted the blade. The thought of Slice and Cassie together sickened me. Even though I'd torn up the number, now that he was done with me, he could always ask my mother for it again and claim he lost it. Or maybe, he'd saved it before he allowed me to tear the paper into bits and pieces.

My gaze misted and I blinked rapidly. "I don't think Cassie will ever leave Chad."

I wouldn't break down over Slice, especially in front of my mother.

"She just hasn't met the right guy." She turned around to face me. "Slice might be it."

One look at my face and she froze. I tensed, preparing for the onslaught of questions. Yet, they didn't come. Instead, she wrapped her arms around me and pulled me close. After a moment, I relaxed, snuggling against her. A stray tear escaped my eye, which I quickly swiped away. No matter how old I got, her embrace would forever be a healing balm. There's nothing like a mother's love, as the saying goes.

I sniffled.

"Oh, sweetie, don't cry. Cassie will come to her senses, one day," she murmured, pressed a kiss to my forehead, and pulled away. "Get some rest, Effie. We have a long day tomorrow."

She rose, shed her dress, and went to the bathroom, leaving me alone on the bed.

For years, my mother's ditziness and hyperfocus on fixing Cassie's dumpster fire of a life blinded her to my emotions, and the reasons behind them. This time was no different.

I pushed back the covers and laid down. Staring at the ceiling, I willed my mind to quiet. To forget. Without a doubt, the signing would be rough and test my strength. Yet, I'd get through it, and never again allow someone like Slice into my heart. Never again would I chase a man because of a girlish fantasy I'd cooked up. From here on out, I'd focus on myself, on my studies, on being my mother's part-time author's assistant. Love would be a future endeavor—if it was even destined for me.

And yet, despite my silent pledge, the memory of Slice's touch lingered. Tears streaming down my cheeks, I drifted into a restless sleep.

SLICE

Dickheadness and miserable motherfuckery tended to keep a man awake at night. Once Effie left, I didn't sleep one goddamn wink. Zero. Zilch.

Fucking *nada*.

That door slam lived on repeat in my head, competing with replays of my evening with Effie. I went over all our interactions from the moment we met a year and a half ago until the moment I finally took her in my arms. A few irrefutable facts settled into my brain. One, she'd wanted to fuck me and asked no questions. The tit pic entered my evidence.

Yeah, it was to alleviate my fucking guilt, but I clocked it as a win for me. Two, *she* never once told me she wanted something more. I thought we were on the same page. Had I known—had she opened her goddamn mouth *beforehand*—I would've kept my cock in my pants.

A flaming fucking lie, but whatever. This was about making my pain go away, not finding a way to agree with her take on the situation.

Three, she had a helluva lot of goddamn motherfucking nerve shoving all the blame on me. I didn't force her. I didn't make any promises. *And* I'd pulled away from her weeks ago. *She* was the one determined to have me.

The more I justified my position, the more sleep eluded me. Too many times to count, I had to stop myself from texting her. Several times, I picked up my phone, hoping to find a message from her. By the time the sun rose, I felt meaner than a fucking bear and lower than a goddamn snake.

At the last event, Daria paid for my accommodations for the night before the signing and the night of. This year, she threw in an extra day for me, and I was grateful. I couldn't imagine having to face Effie the morning after I'd been such an asshole.

After a quick shower, I felt marginally better. Concerned I might run into Effie in the restaurant, I opted for a drive-thru meal. Quick, greasy, and filling. Once I parked, I dug in. The cup of Joe was weaker than I liked, but it had to do until I straightened this shit out. Maybe, later, I'd find a nicer restaurant for us, so we could talk like grown-ups instead of school kids flinging accusations and blame. Neither one of us had been upfront and now we were suffering.

An irrefutable truth of my own? I didn't want to lose Effie. Her friendship. She wasn't mine to lose. I didn't want her to be mine. Not at all. Never in a million years. She was young, sweet, and disappointingly innocent. Though she'd had two lovers, she still expected roses and romance...

Romance?

Romance.

Just because she wasn't mine—and I didn't want her to be—didn't mean I couldn't steal her away after tonight's dinner, and wine and dine her. Daria paid for our tickets, so she, Effie, and I would sit at the same table. Readers were attending as well, but I could whisper sweet nothings to Effie in between talking to everyone else.

Romance wasn't my specialty. When I had a woman, she never wanted for shit. Except, *maybe*, sweet nothings outside the bedroom. Even that was debatable. I laid good dick and feasted on her pussy. If I couldn't find poetic words, I was forgiven.

Effie required more. She needed romance, and her mom's books would help me.

Grinning like a lunatic, I walked across the parking lot to the trash can right outside the restaurant's entrance. Before returning to the hotel, I stopped at *Barnes and Noble* to purchase a copy of Daria's latest book. Should've done that days ago since my appearance centered around her male lead— Moose. I could've bought the copy from Daria. That risked running into Effie. Just deciding to read the book would also reflect badly on my fucking ass. Besides, when the corporate office contacted Daria and informed her that her books were approved for sale in their physical stores, Lennon called me. He told me to tell everyone to go to their local *Barnes and Noble* to buy her book, so they'd turn a profit and continue to be offered on shelves.

Back in my hotel room, I glanced at the blurb on the back cover of *Ink & Iron*.

Bestselling romance author Darcy Mouton knows how to write passion, betrayal, and redemption—but nothing in her carefully crafted stories prepared her for Colt "Moose" Lawson. The infamous enforcer of the Red Reapers MC is everything she shouldn't want: dangerous, untamed, and haunted by a past that has left blood on his hands.

When Darcy finds herself tangled in the club's world, researching a novel she never intended to live, Moose becomes both her protector and her greatest temptation. Their connection is raw and undeniable, but as secrets unravel and enemies close in, Darcy must decide if she's willing to risk everything—including her heart—for a love that was never meant to have a happy ending.

Because in Moose's world, love isn't written in ink. It's carved in flesh. And the price of forever might just be death.

What the absolute fuck?

No. Just fuck no.

Chuckling without humor, I shook my head in denial. Reread the blurb.

This woman—

Was she—

Fuck me! Had Lennon read this bullshit? Had Effie? Yes, and probably. A slight weight lifted off my shoulders. If they hadn't had a problem or saw the obvious, then I was overreacting.

Fuck it. It was Daria's goddamn book. I hadn't bought it to pick it apart or even to learn about Moose. I'd bought it to help me smooth things over with Effie.

Sighing, I stretched out on the bed, pretending I didn't notice the lingering scent of Effie's body wash on my pillows, and opened the book.

I'd never seen a more beautiful man. His head of chestnut brown hair fell to his waist, and I longed to run my fingers through that living silk. His smooth, youthful face reminded me how many years separated us. I'd never pictured myself as a cougar, but I fell head over heels the moment I met him. For the first time since my divorce five years ago, I realized it was the right decision. It hadn't been mine and I'd begged Linx not to leave me. I'd begged him to come back. Essie, Candi, and Holt sided with me…

Scowling, I snapped the book shut.

Linx, Essie, Candi, and Holt? Was she shitting me? That was too fucking close to Lennon, Effie, Cassie, and Heath for my fucking comfort.

Goddamn it!

The novel felt hot and heavy in my hand. I wanted to pitch the motherfucker against the wall and never open it again. No, I wanted to bleach my brain and forget what the fuck I'd read.

Effie, I reminded myself. I was doing this for Effie.

I'd tear off the bandage and skip to the romance. Probably chapter two or three. Generally, the first chapter or two set up the meet-cute, yada, yada, yada.

> *His tongue speared into my juicy pussy, and I threw my head back in ecstasy, riding his face and screaming. My needy clit brushed against his nose, and I rode him faster. I squeezed my nipples past the point of pain, lost in his tongue bath.*
>
> *"Moose!" I cried, grinding harder, near a catastrophic explosion. I'd never been so fucking wet. I'd never wanted to suck a man off and swallow every drop of his cum as much as I did Moose.*

Jesus Christ. The woman was fucking insane.

> *I didn't want his pussy eating to end, but I'd die from the pleasure if he didn't stop, and*

I refused to end it until I came all over his face. He slid two fingers up my asshole, and I shattered. My pussy gushed, my eyes rolled back in my head, and I wailed. I fell to his side, my entire body trembling. But my man, my big bad biker babe, didn't give me a chance to catch my breath. He stretched his long, muscular frame over little old me, parted my thighs, and slammed into me.

I tipped my head back and keened in ecstasy.

"Fuck me! Fuck me harder!" I snarled, the animal in him bringing out the one lurking in me. "Fuck this pussy raw!"

Long, rough fingers grabbed my ankles and shoved them above my head. His big, thick cock buried balls deep in my hot hole, stretched me.

"Whatever you want, darlin'."

His Southern accent was—

His Southern *what*?

Fuck. I was getting what I deserved, not reading the books she always gushed about. Not only would I have to bring out my inner Southern boy, but I'd have to talk to a woman who longed to fuck me while claiming she wanted to set me up with her daughter. One of her daughters. I'd already hooked up—

The ringing phone interrupted my spinning mind. I threw the novel aside and snatched my phone from the nightstand, smiling when I saw 'Dad' on the screen.

"We're good?" I asked once I answered. No need for pleasantries. I knew why he was calling.

"Negative," Dad said gravely.

I shot into a sitting position. "What the fuck do you mean?"

"They want the fucking money back, son. Riker told them to fuck themselves. He'd already paid them that fucking bounty on your head."

Jesus Christ. "Riker is going to demand blood from me."

"Someone else's," Dad said. "Yours will still be in your fucking body, so look on the bright side."

"What fucking bright side? I've worked hard to stay out of Riker's path as much as possible."

"Too fucking bad, asshole. Should've stole the shit right."

"I worked with what I had," I yelled, my hackles rising. "Riker sent me to Memphis with half a day's notice and on my fucking own."

"Shouldn't have shown your fucking face."

"I broke into their motel room in the middle of the fucking night while they were asleep to minimize risk to myself, Dad. I didn't know those assholes would identify me."

"You wore your fucking cut!"

"I blindfolded those two motherfuckers."

"You should've plucked their fucking eyes out. Couldn't blindfold both of them at the same fucking time, dumb ass. *Or* you shouldn't have worn your cut."

"I don't take off my colors. You taught me that and Riker drilled it into all of us."

"Use your fucking noggin, Slice. You work with what's available to get the job done. It was you, two motherfuckers from a rival club, and their drugs you were there to borrow."

"It's done, Dad. Drugs are in our possession—"

"*Were*," Dad cut in. "Riker sold them far above market value."

"Tell me he didn't fuck with those drugs. Cut the coke with baking soda. Exchange marijuana with plant materials."

"He promised me he wouldn't do that again, boy. Told him I'd turn in my fucking patch before I die over stupid shit."

"Of course you would," I bit out. "Except you can't now. He paid my bounty. He'll expect the Elmont men to kiss his fucking ass and jump ten feet in the fucking air when he snaps his fucking fingers."

"Enough, Slice!" Dad growled. "He's our president and he didn't have to try to save you. He even offered a one percent cut of our earnings to the Sinners. Wasn't enough. They wanted the drugs returned or their buy cost repaid *and* seventy-five percent of the money Riker received."

"Fuck." I blew out a heavy breath. So much could've gone wrong during that meeting and I would've lost my father and brother. "I'm glad you and Drifter made it out safe. And Riker," I hastily added before Dad got on my ass.

"Sumbitches kept to their fucking word and let us walk on and leave club grounds unscathed. Your bounty is paid. Now they just want you fucking dead. Even if Riker wanted to hand over the drugs, he couldn't."

Despite what Dad believed, I'd bet my ass Riker fucked with the merchandise before he sold that shit. Striker's claim that Dutch was in the area came to mind. Arguing with my dad over Riker wouldn't help, so I relayed the information.

"Goddamn it. Those rotten motherfuckers!" Frustration filled Dad's voice and he blew out a heavy breath. "Lay low. Understand? Don't leave your fucking room except to go down to the fucking signing—"

"It's not in the hotel," I interrupted. "Tonight's dinner is."

"Fuck. Knew this was a bad fucking idea, Slice. You're not a goddamn model; you're a motherfucking biker. Keep your eyes and ears open on the way to that place tomorrow since I already know you'd decline having Striker send some of his boys. Strength in numbers, you know?"

Striker wouldn't agree anyway, but I didn't point that out.

"Yeah, Dad. I'm declining the offer. It'll bring more attention to me. I don't want to put Effie in danger."

That slipped out before I realized it.

A moment of silence went by. "Thought that woman's name was Daria."

"Effie's her daughter," I said with a sigh.

"She knows about you?"

"Some. Not that it matters. It was just a fling. She's too fucking young for me."

"How old?"

"Twenty-one. As I said, too fucking young."

Dad's counting annoyed me. "I consider myself reasonably educated, boy," he finally said. "You're twenty-seven. I think you're about six years older than her. Not a big age difference."

"It doesn't matter, Dad," I snapped. "It's over. We hooked up and I sent her on her way. She hates my fucking guts, but she's Daria's assistant. She'll be there."

"Good. As long as no one can connect her to you, she's safe."

"I took her dancing," I admitted. "At the club," I added. "Introduced her to Striker. I claimed her to cut down on the bullshit."

"Fuck, let me call Striker. Tell him you two had a big blow up and you ended things. She wanted more than you could give. Might be a lie, but don't want that sumbitch accusing you of pulling the wool over his eyes."

Dad didn't know how close to the truth he'd come.

"Meanwhile, stay in that fucking room until it's time for the signing. Before I left OKC, I called a president from another club. Unaffiliated with us, but not our enemies. Asked him to send any brothers he can spare to assess the situation. Don't completely trust Striker, anyway. As for Riker, don't be so hard on him. He's a little high-strung, but he's an okay motherfucker if you know the right words to say to him."

Or threw enough money at him. Riker saved me, so my annoyance should've made me feel like a selfish prick. But, nope. Riker was a motherfucker.

"After I call Striker, I'm going to call the other president and see if his brothers are on the way. If so, how close they are to arrival."

"Okay, Dad." My idea to smooth things over with Effie was blown to hell. Tonight was my only chance to do so. Tomorrow, we'd be so fucking busy and there'd be so many people around—including her mother—I wouldn't get the chance. "Anything else?"

"Remember: order room service. Don't go to whatever fucking dinner you mentioned. Stay the fuck in that room, son," Dad reiterated. "You're in serious shit. When that signing thing is over, get to Striker's. Drifter and Riker kept on to Vegas. I need to give them a head's up, so they don't run into trouble on the road. Hang tight. I'll be there in time to ride back to OKC with you Saturday night."

After ruining my fucking day, my father disconnected.

Effie

"Rise and shine, valentine!" my mother blared, shaking my shoulder until I cracked my eyes open.

I'd gotten little sleep last night or the night before when I'd stormed from Slice's room. Combined with the emotional turmoil of rejection and the physical strain of being put through a mattress night before last and suffering dejection and disappointment at Slice's no-show last night, I was exhausted. Emotionally. Physically. Mentally. I'd intended to sleep until the signing started, counting on Slice to help my mother set up. Alas, Mom had different plans, bright-eyed and bushy-tailed despite her second night of drinks and staying up until the early morning hours. After the dinner ended, I came up to the room. Mom partied.

Hangovers were an affliction my mother had never suffered from, a gift my sister was bestowed with, but one that skipped my brother and me. I suppose we inherited Dad's genes. He suffered after a night of drinking.

Uncle Mike complained Dad was a teetotaler even on their fishing trips. Dad looked forward to time with his brother. He didn't need drinking to enjoy himself.

While Mom socialized, I talked to Dad for an hour. Part of that time, he gushed about Mom's night at Red Rum. More than likely, she'd handed him the same spiel as me. Even if I'd ratted her out, Dad wouldn't have believed me over her.

Moving on from that sour fact, I pitied Dad's disappointment at Uncle Mike's last-minute ditching of the fishing trip. They hadn't had such a weekend in months because Mom demanded Dad's time.

"Come on, sweetie. Up, up!" Mom bustled to the window and opened the drapes. "We need to get ready."

Sunlight hit my face, and I recoiled, shielding my sensitive eyes from the brightness. A glance at the clock revealed it was 6:49 AM, eleven minutes before our agreed-upon wake-up time.

"Can't I sleep for ten more minutes?" I asked and yawned.

"Nope! We need to shower, dress, eat, set up, and do our stretches. Well, we should do our stretches first, but you get the point." She breezed to her phone. "We should've gotten up nineteen minutes ago, so you slept in."

"We agreed on 7:00 AM," I reminded her, though I begrudgingly exited my bed.

"Plans change, so look alive," she chirped, a Phoenix Rising song blaring from her phone's speaker. "You know the drill, Effie. Squats, lunges, crunches, planks, and our stretches."

Wordlessly, I turned to face her. We started with twenty standing hip openers, ten on each side. As I dragged my raised leg from right to left, my head bobbed to the music. Phoenix Rising was one of my favorite bands, and Sloane Mason my ultimate celebrity crush. His alluring voice, combined with his talent on the guitar and his bandmates' skills, invigorated me. By the time we moved onto arm circles, some of my tiredness was starting to dissipate. Completing those marked the end of our warm-up, and the beginning of the real workout.

We hadn't packed any of our weights, so we should breeze through.

"Look at you, perking up already," Mom said as I finished my first squat.

"Yeah," I responded simply.

Normally, we used this time to chitchat and plan for our day. As overbearing as she could be, I cherished our bond and enjoyed exercising with her. Yet, Slice had me dejected, and the thought of using my brain for a conversation seemed like a Herculean task. How I'd get through the day, I didn't know. Playing nice with the man who had my heart aching would require academy-award-level acting. All I wanted to do was scream at him for being such a fuckboy and slap myself for my naïveté.

Twenty squats later, we moved onto lunges. One exercise down, too fucking many more to go.

"God, I hate these," Mom groaned, already shaking after two.

Thirty lunges were our standard, fifteen for each leg. This routine was years old, but she still struggled to stay balanced and maintain proper form.

"Only twenty-eight left," I teased, grinning at her glare.

"Don't remind me."

Stuck faded into *Inferno*, Phoenix Rising's most popular song, and a love letter to his controversially young wife. The questionable timeline of their relationship aside, Georgie and Sloane Mason seemed to have a strong bond, and I aspired to have the connection they shared.

How had they done it? How had she known, even under eighteen, that Sloane was *the one*? In interviews, she often mentioned love. How much she loved Sloane and how much he loved her. I still maintained respect was more important and impactful because love rarely lasted. But a connection? A bond? Yeah. That lasted.

I mistakenly believed I was bonding with Slice.

I shook my head to rid thoughts of him. It was bad enough I'd cried myself to sleep again last night. I didn't need to remind myself every five seconds that he didn't want me.

"Thank God that's done," Mom breathed, twisting her body and settling onto the floor.

Huh, I hadn't even realized we were done. Brooding over a guy had its perks. Thirty lunges breezed by.

We moved onto the crunches. We practiced many alternatives of them, depending on the day. Today, I was feeling punch crunches. At home, I did those with dumbbells. Nonetheless, maybe attacking the air would help me feel less mopey.

I adjusted my legs until they were separated by the ideal width. "Punch crunches okay with you, Mom?"

"Yep," she answered. "An extra arm workout is always good by me."

For some reason, Mom hated her arms.

With her confirmation given, we began to move, lifting our upper bodies, holding the crunch, and punching with each fist. Mom's movements were more controlled, while mine were faster and more aggressive. Each time I punched the air, I imagined Slice's stupid face. Not the healthiest coping mechanism, but I'd held myself together by a thread for almost two days. I'd rather drop a dumbbell on my foot than talk about my emotions. Imaginary violence it was.

"You all right, sweetie?" Mom asked near the end of our circuit. "You're going a little hard with those hits."

Shit.

If *she* noticed, I really needed to dial it back.

"Just wanna make up for the junk we'll eat later." Hopefully, the answer satisfied her. "Plus, I have to burn away all the extra food we've eaten on this trip."

Not much more than usual. Yesterday, I had neither the time nor an appetite for most of the day.

Until dinner last night, Mom finished signing books and swag while I saw to last minute preorders and sorted mugs, T-shirts, posters, and lip balm. I'd packed the rolling carts and set up a livestream for Mom, where she'd blasted *Ink and Iron* and preened over Slice on her cover and his appearance at the signing.

The word *bounty* ran through my head—*Striker's* words. But I dismissed it. They weren't concerned so why should I be? I proceeded to post the address of the signing. Sapphire Knight, the event organizer, talented author, and all-around lovely woman, allowed the attending authors to raffle two tickets to readers. Mom told me to include the address in my posts, so I did. I was fairly certain the VIP tickets were sold out. Not many tickets would be available at the door.

Mom grabbed my fists, mid-punch. "Effie, love, I think the fast food is worked off," she said, giggling.

"Right," I panted. I'd exerted a lot of energy into the exercise.

Luckily, Mom believed my explanation with no further questions. She hovered at the wrong times.

I started the punch crunches again.

"Stop, Effie!"

"We eat healthy at home, Mom, but when we travel, it's a different story. I'm trying to burn extra calories."

"I understand," she said, fanning herself. "I'm going straight to my treadmill when we get home."

Halting my fists, I nodded. I missed our at-home gym. Heath had been the one to suggest having the garage double as an exercise room. Once he moved away, we commandeered his equipment, including the giant exercise mat preferable to the hotel floor.

A few seconds of rest, and we moved on to our last exercise and the most grueling of the bunch, a one-minute plank. While lunges were Mom's worst enemy, planks were mine. That sentiment was doubly true today when my body begged for more sleep after two restless nights. Often, I treated this routine as a warm-up and went for a thirty-minute jog once we finished, with extra stretches when I got back. Today, that wouldn't be possible. Even if I had the time, I simply didn't have the energy.

"And done." Mom's announcement always came with flair. She settled onto all fours while I collapsed into a heap. "Cobra now, sweetie."

I grunted, still lying on the carpeted floor.

"Effie, darling, we just have three things left. Cobra, child's pose, and standing wide-legged forward bend. You can be lazy in the shower."

Sighing, I pulled myself into position. I didn't want her to get suspicious, nor did I want to throw off her groove because I went and developed a crush on a playboy biker. Besides, neglecting my body for *him* was doing me a disservice. I wouldn't give him the satisfaction of knowing how much his rejection hurt. I could be depressed when I got home, but today, I'd pretend all was well.

I arrived at the convention center without a hitch. Dad hit the road last night. Riker was allowing Drifter to turn around and head to Austin as well. It was some serious shit if I needed a fucking escort.

When I walked into the ballroom where the signing was being held, I spotted Effie before she saw me. She was stacking books in the middle of her mother's table between a basket wrapped in cellophane and tied with a gold bow and rows of swag bags. On the side of the table, a retractable banner stood with a gigantic photo of Daria superimposed in front of me.

I snorted. I couldn't wait until the event was over. Sometime, in the early morning hours, I decided I probably wouldn't work for Daria again. Hell, today probably marked the end of my modeling career. The sooner I got my ass over there and Effie turned her devastated gaze to me, the sooner I could look toward the end of the day.

Except...

Her gaze wasn't devastated. It was fucking frozen. She looked at me as if she hadn't fallen apart in my arms. Her cold greeting felt as if she cut me with a shard of ice.

"Effie—"

"Mom wants to know if you're willing to sign books if the readers ask."

"Don't I always?"

Effie shrugged. "I'm just relaying the message, Slice," she said briskly.

I stepped closer to her. "We need to talk."

She drew herself up. "I can't imagine what you want to discuss with me."

"Effie—"

"Stop," she gritted, glaring at me. "If we make a scene, we will be escorted out and that won't go over well with my mother. Sapphire has a strict no-bullshit policy, and *you* are reeking of it. If you don't want to get tossed out, dust it off and leave me the fuck alone."

Her chin trembled and her nose reddened, but she swallowed. The frozen glower returned. That one moment of vulnerability gave me a smidgeon of hope. At some point today, I'd make her listen to me.

As the day wore on, faking my fucking grin for readers with no concept of boundaries became more challenging. More than one broad tried to grab my dick and even more groped my chest. The no-touching policy meant very little to some bitches, even if both Effie and Daria reminded them each time they got too handsy.

"Thank you so much," a brunette squealed once Effie snapped a picture with her cellphone, absolutely starstruck by Daria. She'd stammered through her request for a picture, and when Daria agreed, I feared she'd pass the fuck out.

Effie handed the woman her phone back with a smile, though the brunette's attention was still squarely on her mother. Not only was Effie acting as her mother's assistant, but as her photographer, too. She took a fuckton of pictures to post on Daria's social media page, including capturing fan reactions of the moment they met their favorite author and the eye candy she brought along.

"It's no problem...umm...I'm sorry, dear, what did you say your name was again?" Daria asked, settling back in her seat.

"Ophelia," the woman provided, turning her attention to me. She swept me with an appreciative glance and a blush rose in her cheeks. Glancing over her shoulder at the two motherfuckers she'd arrived with, she looked at me again and gnawed at her lower lip. "Umm, can I take a picture with you, too?"

I glanced at Effie, gauging her reaction. Her expression was blank, showing zero evidence of being upset with me or caring about the attention other women showered on me. I'd been stealing looks at her all fucking day, hoping to see...hell, I didn't know what. Another chink in her armor? A smile? I felt like a goddamn simp, clambering for her attention and wanting to sulk each time she denied me. Why, I didn't know. She gave me what the fuck I'd told her I wanted. I should be celebrating because she took my words to heart. Instead, her total shutout drove me up a goddamn wall.

"Are you going to answer her, Slice?" Effie's question snapped me back to the present.

Shit.

I'd been staring at her.

But, fuck, she was gorgeous. Her curls were flowing free today, and her tight black outfit clung to her curves, curves I had the pleasure of seeing in their full glory. Big Boy roused.

I cleared my throat, looking at Ophelia and summoning my grin. I hated fucking speaking in the Southern accent Moose had, all things considered, but Daria insisted on it.

Of course she fucking did.

Thank every deity in existence that none of my club brothers were there, or I'd never live this shit down. Nor would I ever convince Riker that I should be *Slice* instead of Pretty Boy.

"A photo? Well, of course, darlin'," I purred, laying it on a little thicker than needed and dragging my eyes over her figure.

Maybe if Effie thought I found Ophelia attractive, she'd stop acting like an ice queen. However, while Ophelia was pretty in her own right, she couldn't touch Effie.

I must've laid it on a little too thick because one of the broad's friends stalked over. Since Ophelia stepped to Daria's table, the two men remained in the background, content to chat with each other. Now both were glaring daggers at me. What the fuck was I missing? Fuck, at first glance, the three of them seemed like good friends. However, the slightly taller one wrapped a possessive arm around Ophelia's waist.

"Fuck, no, she can't take a picture with you," he growled, wrenching her away with such force she stumbled and his jacket fell open.

"Stop being a fucking entitled asshole, asshole," the other motherfucker chastised, though I barely heard him.

When the asshole's movements briefly opened his jacket, I noticed a motorcycle cut, though the patches were covered by his leather jacket. My eyebrows rose, but I decided not to think too much about it. Once the chick left, they'd be gone, too. A Satan's Sinner wouldn't bring a woman to buy a book. They'd fuck me up.

"I'm fine, Stretch," Ophelia said. She was a pretty woman with chocolate brown eyes and rich brown hair. She smirked at the motherfucker who'd yanked her. "Cash is just jealous."

"Jealous?" Cash barked, his blue eyes narrowing. "The fuck I am. Why the fuck would I be jealous of a pretty face *pretending* to be a bad motherfucker?"

"You sure about that?" I couldn't resist the jab. This motherfucker didn't know jack about me. I nodded to his jacket. "I'll show you mine if you show me yours."

Ophelia lifted on her toes and kissed Cash, then turned and kissed Stretch. I blinked and exchanged a glance with Effie. Shock was written on her face. Pre Effie, I might've been green with envy. Now, I mentally hi-fived their game and moved on...

Wait, *what*?

Amusement danced in Cash's eyes as he focused on me. "Years ago, I would've taken you up on your offer, pretty boy, but I'm happily married." He nodded to Stretch. "*And* in love with our woman."

"Ignore him," Stretch growled to me, although I couldn't think of a fucking thing to say.

I'd never laid eyes on that motherfucker and, yet, he threw *pretty boy* at me as an insult.

Interest lit Daria's eyes. I couldn't imagine what might be going through her head and I didn't want to fucking know.

"You're a throuple?" Effie squeaked.

"Don't say that too loud, princess," Cash drawled, and winked at her.

My hands fisted at my side.

Daria leaned in. "Male-male-female?" she breathed, her eyes bright.

Cash shrugged, uneasiness dropping into his face. "Daria, right?" he asked.

She nodded.

"I can give you several ideas for your novels, but real life is messy, and it isn't tied into a neat little bow."

"Will you charge her?" Effie asked.

Cash dug in his jacket and pulled out a pack of cigarettes. He took one from the pack and prepared to light it.

Ophelia snatched it from between his lips. "You can't smoke in here, Cash."

He grunted again, then shook his head, and frowned at Effie. "Won't charge her. Fee loves her books. Besides, I don't need the fucking money."

"We can all use a little extra money," Daria said.

"Not Cash," Ophelia said proudly. "Neither Stretch."

Stretch kissed her again. "Don't have the deep pockets of the Masons and the McCalls, babe."

"Mason?" Daria said. She nodded to Effie and tittered. "Any relation to Sloane Mason? Effie's in love with him."

"Mom!"

"He's gorgeous," Ophelia said, nodding at Effie in girly commiseration. "Besides Meggie, I've never seen eyes so gorgeous and blue."

"Who is Meggie?" Daria asked.

"My brother's wife," Ophelia answered. "They've been together for almost eighteen years now. I've known Sloane almost as long and I've never decided which one of them has the most beautiful eyes." She grinned. "I'll say him because I find him sexy as fuck."

"If you say that to that fucking asshole, I'm never talking to you again, Fee," Cash said woefully. "His ego is big enough." He looked from Daria to Effie. "He's married to my little sister."

Daria gasped and Effie's hands flew to her mouth.

"Meet us later for drinks," Ophelia said to Effie. "We'll call him and let you talk to him."

"No way!" Effie cried, her eyes round.

"Are you serious?" Daria said. "You'd do that for my Effie?"

"You're my favorite romance writer and you're about to sign my books. The least I can do is introduce Effie to Sloane and Georgie."

"Fine," Cash snapped, back to being a surly motherfucker. "Let's go. I have business to see to."

"Not yet," Ophelia said. "I have to get Effie's number and my books signed." She smiled shyly at me. "And I still want a picture with you."

"Fuck no!" Cash growled.

"Welcome back, asshole," Stretch said, shaking his head.

"Behave, you two." Ophelia's coo broke into my dumbfounded outrage. "I promise I will make you both very happy when we get upstairs."

Cash grunted.

Stretch wrapped an arm around her, brushed his lips over hers again, and nodded at me. "You don't really need a picture with this dude, do you, babe?"

A small smile played on Daria's lips. "Aww, c'mon guys, it's just a picture!"

In control of her excitement, Effie smiled, revealing adorable dimples and fucking glowing despite our argument. Had she truly been that upset in the first place, or was she just that good at hiding her feelings? She hadn't texted me or tried to call me to change my fucking mind about my decision.

She told me she wanted more, then accepted when I said I didn't. Not a text. A call. A fucking visit to my room to seduce me into her way of thinking.

I'll bet she didn't even miss me at the fucking dinner. She'd probably turned her pretty smile on a motherfucker I hated—didn't know his fucking ass but couldn't stand him—charmed him with her wit and opinions, and suggested they keep in contact on the Gram.

That stung the fuck out of me.

"Let the girl live a little," Daria added.

"What the fuck's that mean, lady? Mind your damn business," Cash snapped.

Effie's smile dropped.

I tensed, positioning myself closer to Effie and Daria, and examining the men for weapons. If they *were* bikers, chances were they packed heat.

"Don't talk to her like that, asshole," Effie replied, glaring daggers at the guy.

She tried to step up to him, uncaring that he was bigger than her. Out of instinct, I placed a hand on her shoulder, keeping her in place. She froze, transferring her stare to me before shrugging my hand away. And fuck, did that rejection sting.

Luckily, Stretch spoke up, forestalling further interference.

"Cash, stop being a goddamn jackass and chill out." Sighing, he gave me another dirty glare before looking at Effie and Daria. "Sorry, ladies. We'll go now."

He grabbed Cash's hand and dragged him away.

Ophelia's face was fully red. "I'm sorry."

As she hurried off, I gave her a thumbs up.

Once they walked out of the ballroom, I released a disbelieving laugh.

"That was some bullshit," I said with a shake of my head.

"Some people have no goddamn sense." Effie looked at her mother. "You all right, Mom?"

"I'm fine, sweetie. I wish he had told me his ideas. I'm sure you know Ophelia won't introduce you to Sloane now." Daria shrugged. "If they were telling the truth. I mean, what are the odds."

Effie's shoulders slumped, but she nodded. "You're right, Mom."

Daria placed a hand on her chest. "But Cash was so sexy protecting Ophelia. Oh, swoon! That's how Moose would act over Darcy, so I'll use this as inspiration."

Despite myself, I studied Effie. I wanted her opinion on the matter. Would she want me to be so protective over her? Or would she tear into me, as she'd begun to tear into that prick?

Fuck.

No, I couldn't think like that. Nothing, absolutely nothing, would ever become of me and Effie. She was a good fuck, and that's it. Nothing more. Absolutely nothing more.

Our friendship just had me confused.

Daria's smile returned and a giggle escaped her. "If I'm honest, I was a little jelly. Who wouldn't want a hot guy getting all possessive over them?"

Effie wrinkled her perfect nose. "Eww, Mom."

"Oh, hush. I'm not talking about your father. He'll never make a scene like that in public. In private, though—"

"Oh my gosh, I'm not listening!" Effie screeched, slapping her hands over her ears. "Lalalala!"

Daria laughed, and I couldn't help but join in at the childish display.

"Okay, okay, I'm sorry, darling," Daria said when her daughter dropped her hands. She glanced at her phone, humming. "It's nearly lunchtime. Why don't you two grab a bite to eat?"

Fuck, yes. That would allow me time to speak to Effie, to clarify what I said. I liked her—*really fucking liked her*—but there was a list of reasons why we'd never work. *It's not you, it's me* was a cliché route to take, but in this case, it was pure honesty.

"Ok—"

"I'm not hungry, Mom," Effie interrupted, suddenly tense. "You and Slice go. I'll man the table."

Traffic to her table hadn't been that heavy for the past twenty minutes. Not that Daria noticed Effie's smokescreen.

"Well, okay." She stood from her seat behind the table and looked at me. "Slice—"

"I'll wait." After today, I was sure Effie would block me, ensuring we'd never clear the air. "I'm not that hungry, either."

"Aww, shucks, looks like I'm eating alone." Daria sighed, giving me puppy dog eyes, or at least attempting to. "Come keep me company?"

Effie looked at her mother as if she'd grown two heads, and I found myself unable to say anything.

Because, shit, for someone who claimed to love their husband, she was always a little too flirty. Alternatively, she could be trying to lure me away to talk to me about her other daughter, Bassie. That didn't interest me in the slightest, because it wasn't Bassie I wanted, but her sister.

"You wouldn't want fans to miss their favorite author *and* Moose, would you?" I asked, praying the question sent her away.

Daria deflated but nodded. "I suppose you're right. I'll be right back, then."

She disappeared into the crowd, heading to the breakroom where refreshments were kept.

"You should've gone with her." Effie set her camera down and dropped into one of the seats at the table. "She probably wanted to talk to you about Cassie."

Oh, fuck, that *was* her name. No matter, Cassie, Bassie, Dassie, she didn't interest me. She could be as stunning as her mother and sister, and I wouldn't want her.

"I'm sure you'd love to add another girl to your roster."

"I don't want Cassie, Effie," I murmured, the jab annoying the hell out of me.

She paused, then shrugged. "Then you did good not going with Mom, because she wants y'all together."

"I'm aware, but I don't care. I want—"

"Save it," she interrupted, pinning me with a hard stare. "We don't have to talk, Slice, and you don't have to lead me on. You got what you wanted, and I'm not going to say anything to my mother, so there won't be any drama on that end."

I slammed my hands on the table and caught the attention of a few people nearby. Effie jumped. I closed my eyes and took a breath, willing myself to calm down. She was hurt and had every right not to talk to me, but her dismissive tone and curt words grated on my last fucking nerve.

"I didn't just want to fuck you, Effie." I deliberately stayed quiet to avoid attracting more attention. "I had no intention of fucking you, but—"

"Oh, so I seduced you?" she asked sarcastically. "Poor little you, the big bad college girl using her feminine wiles and dragging you to bed."

Jesus fucking Christ, this girl.

"Don't pretend you weren't sending signals my way all night, and don't pretend to know what I'm thinking," I growled, meeting her glare with one of my own. "I like you, Effie. I liked fucking you, yes, but that wasn't all it was. I enjoyed your company, enjoyed talking to you, so don't think you're just a piece of ass."

Finally—fucking finally—she started to soften, vulnerability creeping onto her face. "Then if you like me, why can't we be more?"

Fuck, maybe this was a mistake. Maybe she had the right idea, and I should've left well enough alone. But her ignoring me, and the disdain in her eyes the few times she looked at me, affected my ability to think rationally. Because I wasn't considering anything but fixing the damage I'd done, even if it'd been a necessary move. Perhaps I was a selfish asshole, wanting to have my cake and eat it too, wanting Effie to want me even while I knew the complications that being with her would bring.

"Well?" she whispered, the hope in her eyes tangling me the fuck up.

Sighing, I ran a hand through my hair. Even if the thought of making Effie mine appealed to me, she wasn't my ol' lady. Maybe once the bounty on my head was dealt with, I'd come clean and lay everything out for us to have a shot at something serious. But for now, I'd give her a watered-down version of the truth.

"My lifestyle isn't cut out for a girl like you, babe." A million scenarios flashed through my mind. They all involved Effie hurt if I staked my claim. "Believe it or not, I'm just trying to protect you."

She laughed, devoid of humor. "That isn't for you to decide. I'm a grown woman, Slice, capable of making my own decisions. Stop acting like my parents and babying me because you don't want to admit the truth. You don't want anything serious with me, so don't bullshit me. It hurts, but I'll get over it."

For fuck's sake, was she not listening to me? If she could read between the lines, the conversation would be much simpler.

"Goddamn it, Effie—"

"Save it, Slice." The mask she'd been wearing all day slipped back in place. "It's better if we just keep things professional and forget about our lovemaking."

"I don't want—"

This time, it wasn't Effie who interrupted me, but her mother.

"What's going on here?" Daria asked, her sudden appearance taking me aback.

Shit, but I needed to get it together. If she'd been an enemy, I would be a dead motherfucker, all because I was hung up on the pretty little thing seated before me.

"Nothing, Mom." Effie stood and reclaimed her camera. "Slice and I were just talking."

Perhaps I hadn't given Daria enough credit, because she looked ready to call bullshit. Her eyes flickered between me and Effie, brows furrowed. "Talking about what?"

"Stuff," I grumbled, my already shitty mood plummeting. "I'm ready to eat now."

Before either woman protested, I strolled away. My appetite still hadn't appeared, but I needed a breather, needed to get away from my overbearing boss and her infuriating minx of a daughter.

Most of all, I needed a goddamn drink, and for my feelings for Effie Monroe to fucking disappear.

Effie

Sometimes, I wondered if my mother's ditziness was an act for people to underestimate her. Ever since Slice returned from lunch, Mom eyed me suspiciously and cast dirty looks at him, as if she had somehow picked up on what happened between us. Maybe it was tiredness, but she seemed tense and snappy. With fans, she was her usual bubbly self. But the moment her adoring admirers departed, she gave us the cold shoulder. I would ask her about it, but I didn't want to raise her hackles even more. So, if she didn't bring it up, neither would I.

Quarter to four, my hunger reared itself. I hadn't eaten a single thing all day. My cheeks heated at how loudly my stomach growled. Mom went to the breakroom once, and Slice had gone twice, plus he'd taken a bathroom break. For some reason, his frequent departures annoyed me, as did the hungry eyes that followed him. I wasn't blind or dumb; I knew other women wanted him. But that didn't stop my irritation, especially whenever he rewarded his admirers with his handsome grin or a cheeky wink.

Fucking asshole.

My one bright spot today had been the almost meeting of Sloane Mason. Even that disintegrated in a cloud of fuckery.

My stomach growled again. Both Mom and Slice looked at me, worsening my embarrassment.

"That's my sign to eat." I set my camera aside. "I'll be quick."

"Okay." Mom glanced away.

Slice merely nodded. The chilly responses from them worsened my mood. Tiredness turned me bitchy enough. Combined with my hunger and the unspoken tension, I wanted to scream. Before I said something I regretted. I stormed off.

Halfway to the breakroom, I detoured. There were loads of books I wanted to purchase, but Mom balked every time I tried to excuse myself. I was there as an assistant not a reader.

Now, the crowd swallowed me. I couldn't see Mom or Slice, so they couldn't see me.

What was a little hunger if it meant buying a few books *and* having them autographed? Perhaps, I couldn't visit twenty authors, but Andi Rhodes and Jessa Aarons? Definitely.

Praying their tables were on this side of the ballroom, I marched along, waving at some authors I knew from previous signings and hoping neither of them had long lines. The signing ended at five, so I didn't have much time left to make my own haul.

Andi's banner met my happy gaze, and I grinned, hurrying to her table and grateful a fan brushed by.

"Hi, Effie," she greeted.

My head snapped up. "You know my name?" I squeaked.

She grinned and nodded. "You're Daria's girl. Besides, it's on your name tag."

Heat rose in my cheeks, and I glanced down, swallowing. "Right," I mumbled.

"No biggie," she assured me with a bright smile, easing my nerves at once.

Until my stomach growled, and I cringed. "I'm starving, but I have devoured every Soulless Kings book you've released. Marble Falls. Washington—"

"Well—"

"Confidentially," I babbled, never handling anxiety well, "from a huge fan to a favorite author, you should really write a series about Black Savages MC, although old dude in *Fender* was such a creeper. By the way, loved the name Fender and Charlie was so badass." I snapped my fingers and glanced at her table. Nearly all her books were sold. I spotted a display copy of *Fender*. The *only* copy I saw. "I will sell my sister for that copy of *Fender*. Never mind. She'll probably want Chad to be a part of the deal and his ass would definitely devalue her worth."

"Are you through, hun?" she asked around laughter.

"Totes," I pushed out.

"Another series that I'm a part of is set in Washington, Effie, not Soulless Kings," she explained. "Those books are set in Oregon and Texas—Marble

Falls. I love your enthusiasm and I'm happy to tell you I wrote Donovan's book. *Forever Savage.*"

"I missed a Black Savages release? How?" I cried, totally bummed. I prided myself on staying up to date with the releases of my favorite authors. My stomach growled again. That bastard would not behave. I gritted my teeth.

"Why don't you grab a bite to eat, Effie? I'll—"

"Nope," I interrupted. "I'm not leaving without Fender. The book, I mean. *Look* at him." I nodded to the model on the cover. "Complete man candy."

"I agree." Andi reached over and grabbed the book. "No need to sell your sister." She beamed at me and grabbed a Sharpie. "Tell me how to spell your name?"

Once I completed the transaction and she signed the book, Andi bagged my book and added cool swag. She was quite helpful and directed me to Jessa's table since I absolutely refused to find food until I sought her out.

I didn't read mafia books as much. Bikers and rockstars were my thing and damn did she have bikers. By the time I reached Jessa's table, my energy had dipped to zero. Probably because I still hadn't eaten. Before I walked up to her, I paused and drew in a few deep breaths to calm myself. I *would* not ramble the way I had with Andi. *And* I'd remember I wore a fucking name badge.

Smiling, I sailed to the table, happy to see two copies of *A Biker's Tiny Present* but not many other books left. "Hi Jessa," I said brightly. "When I saw Tiny's name, I thought it was because he had a tiny peen. I'm so glad I was wrong. He was hung, wasn't he? I was like 'go, girl. Yay, you. And the way they loved Nicky...'"

She blinked and I squinted. I could not believe what the fuck came out of my mouth.

"Er—"

She, like Andi, burst into laughter. I couldn't help myself—I laughed, too.

"I'm sorry. All of that came out wrong."

"It's okay," she assured me. "I'm so glad you enjoyed Tiny's story."

"I did. It was short but it packed such a punch." My motherfucking stomach growled again. "My mother writes encyclopedias. Like, really. Eight, nine hundred pages." I shook my head. "I love her imagination, but I think you should save the two-ton tomes for the penultimate book in the series."

"I get what you mean," Jessa responded. "But I like a combination. Short and sexy *and* long and spicy."

Slice's length came to mind and I wanted to die of mortification. First, that asshole didn't deserve one moment's consideration. Neither him nor his dick. Secondly, I was *over* him. He didn't want me, so I didn't want him.

My stomach growled for the millionth time and I gave up trying to ignore it.

"Let's get your book signed, so you can find something to eat."

I smiled at her. "Thank you, Jessa," I said, drawing in a deep breath to tamp down the raw pain of Slice's rejection. Sating my need for food would help my perspective. "You and Andi have been the best. I appreciate it so much."

"Any time, love," she told me.

I'm sure my mother was ready to send out the National Guard for my ass. Once I finished my transaction and collected my book and more swag, I went to Mom's table and set my purchases on my chair.

"Where were you?" Mom screeched.

"Buying books," I answered. "Now, I'm really going for food."

Not allowing her or Slice a chance to respond, I rushed off.

I found only Leah Kaylen in the breakroom. Leah was an author stationed near my mother's table. Turned out, she was a fan of Mom's work, and was inspired to write her own MC series after reading the books. She'd been nice when she'd introduced herself to Mom, so when she smiled at me as I entered, I offered one of my own, happy to see a friendly face. I wouldn't be a bitch to some random woman for something that didn't involve her.

"You're Daria's daughter, right?" Leah asked as I filled my plate with little sandwiches.

"Yep. Her youngest one," I answered, then took a much-needed bite of food.

I nearly groaned in delight at the taste of cold cuts, cheese, and Italian bread. I could do without the lettuce and tomatoes, but right now, I appreciated every bit of sustenance.

"Ah, thought so. She introduced you as her assistant, but I was like, you two are damn near identical," she said with a laugh, popping a chip into her mouth.

Again, I copied her, forcing a laugh even though I found nothing amusing. "Yeah, I get that a lot. My siblings took after our father, but her genes were stronger for me."

She nodded. Perhaps I'd stop by her table before returning to Mom's. Maybe, I'd take a tour of the entire convention center, instead of dealing with

Slice's brooding stares and my mother's accusatory glances.

"Girl, that's a good thing. Your mama looks good, so you know you're gonna age well too."

A genuine smile spread across my lips. Compliments always lifted my mood. "I hope so, because my daddy's side of the family leaves a lot to be desired."

Leah laughed again, harder than last time. Real giggles escaped me at the boisterous sound. I could bring her to Mom's table so she'd spread some good vibes and allow the final hours of the convention to be enjoyable.

Once our chuckles faded away, we fell into silence, focusing on our food. Fine by me. Even though the friendly conversation helped, idle chitchat wasn't high on my list of priorities.

"Oh, girl, I saw you and that model earlier." Leah wiggled her dark eyebrows and broached a subject I'd rather ignore, especially as I chowed down on my third delicious sandwich. "Y'alls discussion was mighty heated. What's the tea?"

And just like that, my annoyance returned.

"Just a disagreement." I finished my sandwich and debated what to do with the remaining two.

The mere mention of Slice destroyed my appetite. I couldn't get *one* raggedy man and Ophelia what's her face had two. I'd heard about throuples, but I never actually met such a trio. They seemed genuinely happy, even if Cash was an asshole. I wondered what he did for a living. Certainly, if he *was* Georgie Mason's brother, a Google search would provide answers.

By deduction, I reasoned his name was Cash McCall, since Mason was Georgie's married name, and he'd mentioned both.

"A disagreement?"

"Yep."

"Not. Spill, girl."

"Nothing to spill."

Leah snorted. "Sounded like you and that biker had a lover's quarrel."

"Nope. Just had a disagreement." That was my story and I'd stick to it.

"Really?" Mom swept into the breakroom. "You and Slice had a disagreement?" She looked between me and Leah, who must've sensed the energy shift because she hurried the hell out. "What about?"

I blinked, wondering how long Mom had been lurking in the shadows like fucking Batman, eavesdropping on my conversation. Nothing of essence was said, but it was the principle.

"He didn't like a picture I took of him."

The lie came easily. As the youngest daughter, I was babied to the point of suffocation. The skill of lying was a crucial one if I wanted even a little freedom.

Her eyes narrowed. "Slice doesn't seem like the vain type."

"He's literally a model. They're all vain."

"You know better than to stereotype an entire group, Effie Monroe."

"How long had you been listening?" I demanded, wondering if she'd followed me to the breakroom, and for some God-forsaken reason, decided not to alert me to her presence.

"Drop the tone, Effie," she snapped, stepping closer to me. It took a lot to get her angry, but when she was, everyone in her vicinity suffered. "Whatever you're hiding is safe, but I want to know what it is."

Oh, so that's why she followed me. She was taking a page from Slice's book and cornering me for verbal harassment.

"I'm not hiding anything."

"I beg to differ."

"That isn't my problem."

If looks could kill, I'd be a smoldering pile of ash.

"You know what I think?" she started, continuing before I answered her rhetorical question. "I think you're sweet on Slice, and you're bitter that I *know* Cassie is better for him. I didn't see it before—I don't know how—but I do now."

Well, fuck. Color me surprised; she was spot on. Thankfully, she was missing core parts of the story. If she was so worked up over me having a simple crush on Slice, she'd implode if she knew all we'd done.

"So, you're mad because I might have a crush?" I asked, proud of how uninterested I sounded. I couldn't let her know how accurate she was.

"No, I'm mad because I think you hit on him. You have your ass on your shoulders because he rejected you, so you didn't get the expected results from your little stunt. Shame on you for trying to ruin your sister's happiness."

"Shame on you for trying to control everyone's life," I bit out, the words escaping before I stopped myself. "I'm a grown woman, just like Slice is a grown man with free will, so what happens between me and him isn't your business."

Surprise flashed across her face, before her anger returned. "I see. Something *did* happen. I can't believe you'd betray your sister. I thought you were better than that."

"She literally has a boyfriend! And if she hasn't left Chad for all the shit he's done, what makes you think she'd be swayed away by a pretty face?" I retorted, struggling to keep my voice down.

Typically, I tried to placate Mom when she was upset at me. I didn't like it when we argued, and I especially hated how both she and Dad treated me like the Wicked Witch of the Southwest after our fights. But today, of all the days, I couldn't keep my mouth shut.

"Maybe if you hadn't assigned archetypes, you wouldn't be blind to the fact that Cassie won't fucking leave Chad," I continued, words I longed to say for so long spilling forth. "Maybe if you didn't want to control every fucking thing, we wouldn't be having this goddamn conversation!"

I was opening a can of worms that would be impossible to close. My raised voice dawned on me. And yet, her slap still shocked me. It seemed to shock her, too. For a second, neither of us said anything, and neither of us moved. A barrage of curse words was on the tip of my tongue, but instead of saying any of them, I tossed my paper plate onto the floor and shoved past her.

"Get back here!" she shouted, but I ignored her.

I breezed past the few onlookers who had gathered and didn't spare Slice a second glance when I stomped past Mom's stupid fucking table.

"Effie?" Slice called. He followed me, but I didn't answer, so he grabbed my wrist. "Sweetheart, what's wrong?"

The urge to cry suddenly came over me. I looked away, wanting my eyes to stay dry. I was always an emotional crier: my tears came whenever an emotion became too intense. Sometimes, it was good, like during happy occasions and joy overtook me. Today, the reason was positively horrendous. At that moment, I just needed to be alone and decompress.

When the signing ended, I'd clear the air with my mother, but for the time being, staying around people was too daunting.

"I-I just need a breather," I mumbled, tugging my wrist away and running off before he spoke again.

I quickly exited the convention center, squinting as sunlight hit my eyes. The Texas sun was still high in the sky. A breeze blew around me, drying my cheeks as fast as my tears fell. Sniffling, I started off, mindlessly following the sidewalk. I had no destination in mind, intending to roam until I calmed a bit.

Unfortunately, a big hairy hand clamping around my mouth ruined that plan.

A scream left me, and I began to struggle, biting down on whoever was dragging me away. I realized I'd wandered into a more run-down, quiet part of the city, a prime location for nefarious deeds.

"Bitch!" my kidnapper barked, handling me even rougher.

I dug my heels in, prepared to fight to the death if I had to. I didn't know what the man's intentions were, but I *did* know that if he succeeded in getting me to a second location, my chances of survival dropped drastically.

"Drug the slut already," another man ordered.

I scanned the area to gauge the number of opponents. Unfortunately, the two men who accosted me blocked my view.

"*You* have the damn syringe!" bad guy number one replied.

I stomped his foot and he growled, his hold on me loosening.

Another bite of his hand earned my freedom. Adrenaline surged through me, and I broke into a run, never more thankful for my regular jogs than I was at that moment.

"Help me! Help!" I screamed, hoping to capture someone's attention. Recalling what I'd been taught as a child, I started yelling, "Fire, fire, fucking fire!"

My desperate shouts infuriated those who targeted me. "Fucking stop her!"

For a brief, precious moment, I thought I'd get away, that someone would hear me and come to my aid. A body slamming into mine thwarted that hope, knocking me onto the concrete and stealing the wind from my lungs. Pain exploded through my body. Before I screamed again, he shoved a gag into my mouth and kept it in place with a beefy hand. Something was tied around my wrist and a terrified sob bubbled up. The man settled on top of me and I writhed on the ground, trying to buck him off.

Awful outcomes ran through my head. My body found on the side of the highway, and my parents notified of my brutal death. Being beaten and raped, left for dead, and vulnerable to other psychopaths. Kidnapped, sold to the highest bidder, made into some sicko's sex slave. I'd be lucky if this was a mere robbery by some crooks with anger issues, but I doubted it was so simple.

"For fuck's sake, stay still," one of them growled, grabbing a fistful of my hair and shoving my face into the concrete.

Stars danced in my vision, and a sickening thud echoed through the alleyway. When the fuck did we get in an alleyway? Shit, but my head was pounding. I hoped my nose wasn't broken. Blood dripped from it, staining the ground beneath me red. By the time he jabbed the needle into my neck, I was too out of it to care.

As darkness claimed me, I was relieved the pain radiating through me faded.

SLICE

"What the fuck happened?" I demanded upon Daria's return.

One moment, Effie left to eat, and Daria claimed to be thirsty, and the next, sweet Effie hurried past me with tears in her gorgeous eyes. It didn't take a genius to guess that her mother was the reason she was so upset.

"I should be asking you that," she snarled, her furious glare taking me aback. "Did you have sex with my daughter?"

Shit.

Fuck.

Goddamn.

Did Effie tell? *Impossible!*

Why the hell would she tell her mother, after promising she wouldn't? No, she wouldn't do that. Daria made a lucky guess, and I wouldn't incriminate myself by telling the truth. Whether Effie had spilled the beans or not, confessing would lead to other fucking problems.

"Excuse me? Sex with *Effie*?" I pretended outrage at the very suggestion, though I ached to hold her in my arms again. See her gaze soften and look at me as if I owned the fucking world. "You're out of your mind."

"Don't play dumb—"

"Is that why you sent your daughter running off in tears during a professional event? Because you think I fucked her?" I asked, solidifying my dislike for Daria.

I suspected the bullshit she handed me about Effie being too good for me hid the real reason she'd warned me away. Maybe, she sincerely wanted me to contact her other daughter, but Daria Monroe hid a wealth of jealousy for her daughter that she masked as concern.

Not only was she a dumb bitch, but a malicious one, too. Even without all the *other* bullshit, after *this* bullshit, I'd be hard-pressed to work another gig for her. She had the decency to look guilty, but she still wouldn't back the fuck down. I suppose that was where Effie got it from.

"She knows I want you with Cassie and that seducing you was wrong—"

"Stop right there." I couldn't believe the words coming from her mouth. This was not the Daria I'd met before, and certainly not the woman Effie praised. "She didn't seduce me, and no matter what happened, that didn't give you the right to cause a scene because of what your grown fucking daughter did!"

I took a deep breath, trying to suppress the rage and disgust flowing through me at the thought of anyone hurting Effie, of fucking blaming her for an act that took *two* willing participants.

"Fuck this," I muttered, turning on my heel, intending to search for Effie and comfort her.

"You could be sued for breach of contract if you step out that damn door, Slice!" Daria's threat stopped me dead in my tracks.

We were causing a fucking scene, risking being kicked out if shit got any more out of hand. And yet, that didn't phase me one bit.

Daria stepped closer, more composed. "I don't think you want the law involved," she continued, quieter. Her voice trembled. "So please, let's just finish the convention, and then you're free to go where you please."

Damn it all to hell, but she was right. The last thing I needed was a civil suit over some dumb shit. A lawsuit could lead to more discoveries, not only fucking over myself but my brothers and family.

"I'll pay you an extra five hundred," she offered as if cash was the issue here.

Yet, money never hurt. I could use it for gas, some good weed, or to buy Effie a nice gift and properly apologize. The thought swayed me, and begrudgingly, I resumed my spot by the table.

The rest of the convention went by in a blur, and the glances cast by the other attendees grated on my nerves. I checked for messages from Effie to an obsessive degree, disappointment and worry coursing through me each time I came up empty.

What did I expect? She hadn't texted me in two fucking days.

Once we were free to leave, I was out of there. As I hightailed it to my bike, I dialed Effie's number. Still no answer. A frustrated growl left me. I couldn't get to the hotel fast enough, and I prayed that she was curled up in her room, safe and sound. A bad feeling had settled in my gut, and I'd learned to trust that motherfucker. Instincts wouldn't lead you astray; they were designed to protect.

"Effie," I called, pounding on her hotel door. "Sweetheart, are you in there?"

I knocked for ten minutes straight to no avail. That bothersome fucking feeling of something being wrong hadn't left and propelled me to kick the goddamn door.

"I'd appreciate it if you didn't cause damage to hotel property, seeing as I'm footing the bill," Daria said, the last person I wanted to fucking see.

"Effie isn't in there." The realization tore me up.

Because fuck, if she wasn't there, where the hell was she? She could be anywhere. I was at a loss as to where to start looking because she wouldn't answer her phone. Maybe I was paranoid, too used to the worst outcome, but something wasn't right. I'd rather throw a fit over nothing, than ignore my instincts.

Daria rolled her eyes. "I'm sure she is. She's just pouting like a child."

Dislike Daria, huh? Nope! It was official; I couldn't stand this fucking bitch.

As she fished out her keycard, I stormed to the elevators. The chiming of my phone halted me. Unreasonable hope flooded my body. It could be anybody, but I hoped like hell it was Effie.

And in a sense, it was.

Only, the sender wasn't her, but a private number. No, she was the subject of the message, tied up and bloodied.

Unknown: Got your girl, Pretty Boy.
Unknown: Shouldn't have fucked with us.

My heart stopped, then sped up. Fear crashed over me, quickly followed by overwhelming fury. Even if the accompanying message didn't give away who'd snatched her, the specifics were easy to piece together.

"Effie isn't in there," Daria called, her voice trembling. I turned; she was feet away, her eyes wide and watery. "I-I tried calling her phone, but she didn't answer. I texted her, and I apologized, but she isn't answering me. She always answers. Why isn't she answering? Jesus, why did I hit her?"

The panic in her voice was palpable, and she was rambling. I knew, because I bet everything I owned she didn't mean for me to hear that last part.

"You what?" I roared, wanting to rage, to hit something, to kill Dutch and whoever else dared to hurt Effie.

Daria burst into tears, her shoulders shaking from her sobs. "I don't know! She cussed at me, and I was so disappointed, and—"

"And now she's gone, and the last goddamn thing she might remember about you is her mother fucking hitting her for living her life." I grabbed Daria's chin and forced her to look at the picture I received. "That's where your daughter's at! And fuck, I don't know *where* that is."

My voice cracked, but Daria's scream snapped me out of it. My course of action was a poor one. She fell forward; I caught her, holding her as she sobbed and pleaded for her daughter's return. But while she begged to a higher power to protect her daughter, I was thinking of all the ways I'd hurt Dutch when I found his miserable fucking ass. I wanted Effie returned safely more than anything, but no matter her condition, Dutch and his goons *would* die. Neither the national president or the Austin president might back me up, but I hoped Dad would.

And if Dutch and the Satan's Sinners cut Effie's life short, their deaths would be a far gorier affair.

Daria

"What the fuck is going on out here?"

Cash's roar seeped into my panicked brain. At first, I thought I was imagining that Texas drawl that had dripped over my senses as he pitched a jealous fit over his woman. Then, he sauntered into view. The patches on his cut blurred, my eyes too filled with tears to read the words.

"Daria?" Ophelia rushed toward me and grabbed my arms. "What's wrong? What's happened?"

"Let's move it out of the hallway," Stretch advised from a doorway several doors from the room I shared with Effie.

Effie. My baby. I stumbled.

"Death Dwellers MC," Slice said as if he was reading. "Fuck. You aren't here by any chance because of a call from Goose?"

"Are you shitting me?" Cash snarled. "You're *Slice*?"

"Get the fuck in this goddamn room, assholes," Stretch ordered in frustration, closer to us. "I can't fucking intercept the cameras of a major hotel chain."

Ophelia placed her arm around me. "Come on, Daria. Let's go to your room and let Cash and Stretch talk to, er—"

"No!" I wailed. "No! They've taken my Effie. I can't..."

If she hadn't held me up, I would've collapsed.

"We can't leave them alone," Cash said, and I wasn't sure who he meant. "If they took her daughter, they can take her for ransom, too."

"Come on," Ophelia said, her voice calm and soothing, when I only wanted to rage against the world. She'd never faced such a scenario. It was easy for her to remain so cool and collected.

I couldn't find words of protest, so I allowed her to lead me to the room where the men were waiting. The moment Stretch used his keycard on the door and held it open, I staggered into the suite.

Another time I would've enjoyed the spacious living area, but not without Effie.

Ophelia guided me to a sofa, piled with books she'd purchased at the signing as well as shopping bags filled with clothes from the local mall.

Slice, Cash, and Stretch were speaking, but their words went over my head. Even when Ophelia brought a cold washcloth to me and insisted that I lie back on the cleared sofa, I couldn't relax or focus.

"It's fine. I promise. They'll get her back."

Ophelia's constant reassurance grated on my nerves.

"It isn't!" My snarl surprised me. Life was to be enjoyed and problems solved. I looked for the positives as much as possible, considering my life of heartache and betrayal. "My baby is gone." I jumped to my feet and pointed at Slice. "Because of *him.*"

If they'd sent *him* that horrendous photo and those awful messages, it *was* his fault.

"Who are you?" I screamed, unhinged. "Who, goddamn it!"

"Lady, sit the fuck down," Cash ordered. "In the fucking future, I suggest you background check the men you hire."

"He's a model. I checked his portfolio."

"Joke's on you," Cash spat. "Slice is a fucking biker. An *outlaw* biker with a bounty on his head."

I staggered back and my stomach heaved. Words formed in my brain but refused to come out of my mouth. It seemed as if my house of cards collapsed in one fell swoop.

"Why take her and not me?" I pushed out. But then I remembered. She and Slice had a situation that someone found out about. I raised my hands. "Never mind. I already know. They think she's your old lady."

"Something that has you green with jealousy," Slice sniped.

Narrowing my eyes, I stiffened. "I beg your pardon?"

"I read your fucking book, Daria. The one about Darcy and Moose of the Red Reapers. The question is did Effie read that? Does she know you're a jealous bitch? Did Lennon read it? I still can't imagine what you hoped to gain by setting me up with your older daughter. A mother-daughter threesome?"

His words twisted my guilt a little deeper, but that last shot took the cake.

"You're a disgusting asshole. Effie's *mine*, Slice. She has a bright future ahead of her. I don't want her with a model who's too pretty for words and has women falling all over themselves." I sat heavily on the sofa. "I don't want to sleep with you, by the way. It happened on paper. That's my agreement with Lennon. Affairs with my book boyfriends."

"You're sick," Slice said, disgusted. "Affairs with book boyfriends? Claiming your daughter all for yourself? Lennon's more pathetic and long-suffering than I thought."

My nostrils flared. "Long-suffering? I beg to differ. In the early years of our marriage, he cheated on me more times than I care to remember. I had nowhere to go and two young children to think about. My mother didn't want me. I only had a high school diploma. Nothing and no one else. Until I met Ezekial. He rented the house next door."

I tried my best not to think about him. Many times I succeeded. Even when I looked at our daughter, I saw myself and not him. When my children were born, I swore I'd be a much better mother to them than mine was to me.

"When I turned up pregnant, Lennon knew the baby wasn't his. He hadn't touched me. He hadn't wanted me..." However I phrased it, the memory was painful. "It had been months. Ezekial was killed before I told him about our baby. I expected Lennon to throw me out and sue for full custody. Instead, he asked me to give him another chance and we went into marriage counseling. Once I started writing, Lenny told me he preferred me having affairs with my book boyfriends than giving myself to another man." I shrugged, defeated and devastated. "He said until he realized another man wanted me, he didn't think he'd ever lose me."

I tipped my head back and blinked, though my tears continued falling. The truth was spilling out of me, a momentary distraction as images of my sweet baby flashed through my mind. I couldn't imagine what my Effie was suffering. I couldn't imagine losing her in the aftermath of our bitter last exchange. As I listened to my story, spoken beyond the walls of a professional's office, I realized I'd morphed into the woman I'd been determined not to become—my mean, bitter, controlling, hateful mother.

I swallowed and stared at a wall, but saw nothing. I weaved tales of passion, love, and happiness because I'd found it in my husband after traveling a long, painful path filled with heartache and mistakes.

"I'm so sorry, Slice. Find Effie for me. Please. I just want her safe and happy and if you make her happy, I don't care."

"She doesn't know Lennon isn't her father, does she?" Slice asked, his tone unreadable.

I shook my head. "Please don't tell her. Lennon adopted her. His name is on her birth certificate."

"She has a right to know. This isn't one of your goddamn books where you can write happily ever afters. This is real fucking life!"

My guilt worsened. Not only had my last words to her—my actions—been so cruel, but I had never admitted the truth to her. I told myself it was to protect her, but it was only to protect my flawed marriage.

Stretch walked back into the room from what I assumed was the bedroom. I hadn't realized he'd left.

A cigarette hung from the corner of his mouth and he carried an iPad.

He held the tablet out to me. "Give me details. Effie's cell phone number and the carrier. Slice's club isn't equipped with the technology I need, so I have to get to a Dweller chapter in Houston. I'm sending this to our private investigator. Hopefully, by the time I arrive at my destination, I'll have a location."

I felt like a limp dishrag. Accusation burned in Slice's eyes. He'd never look at me the same way again. Lennon blamed himself for my transgressions. If he discovered I'd admitted the truth, I didn't know what would happen.

"I'm so sorry, Ophelia," I said quietly. "I guess you've never been subjected to anything so sordid."

Ophelia held my gaze and offered me an understanding smile. "You'd be surprised."

Effie

I'm not sure how long I was unconscious, but I awoke to a massive headache, surrounded by darkness and cold. Grogginess dulled my brain. Even so, I knew I remained in danger. Though I couldn't remember if I'd dreamed, somewhere inside of me I thought I'd been in the midst of a nightmare and when I opened my eyes, I would be in the hotel room. A part of me prayed every waking moment from the time I asked Slice if we were in a relationship to now was a nightmare.

Unfortunately, it was real. A nightmare, yes, but live and in person. I was tied to a chair with my mouth gagged and my hands and feet bound.

I tested how secure I was. My movement caused the chair to scrape against the floor. The sound echoed and I cringed.

"She awakens," a voice murmured, too close for my comfort.

Disorientation removed my spatial awareness. I didn't know if my kidnapper stood in front of me or behind me.

"How's the head and the nose?" He snickered. "You've been out for hours. I thought we overdosed you."

Even if I didn't have something stuffed in my mouth, I wouldn't have spoken.

Footsteps clipped toward me and terror surged into me. I tried to draw in a deep breath, but instead, I felt as if I lost all my air. I imagined the material gagging me and blocking my airway.

A hand landed on my shoulder. I shook, demanding myself to calm down. Panicking wouldn't help. It might do the exact opposite and hasten my death. Overhead light flared to life and I blinked against the intrusion. Once my eyes adjusted, a cavernous room greeted me. I was in a warehouse. The idea chilled me. Before my mom began writing romances, I loved horror novels and crime fiction. Mom and I watched more than our fair share of true crime.

Empty warehouses, bad dudes, and tied up women rarely ended well. Death didn't necessarily frighten me. It was the occurrence that would lead to my death that chilled me. I was young and in good health as were my parents and siblings. I expected us to live long lives. Other than a nightmare here and there, I didn't think about dying.

One more thing to add to my naïveté belt.

A burly man with shoulder-length red hair walked into my line of vision. A long scar ran along his cheek, disappearing into his ginger beard. His eyes reminded me of a tropical ocean—azure; without the warmth, though. He studied me. His gaze landed on my breasts and he licked his lips.

Another dose of panic roared into me. They hadn't blindfolded me. Not good. If they released me, I could identify them. Tears lurking in my eyes slid down my cheeks. Twenty-one should be too young for regrets, but they filled me.

Mom would receive news of my disappearance and remember our last encounter where I'd been so horrible to her. Slice would hear about me and...? I didn't know. I only wished I'd handled the aftermath of our lovemaking better. Our seduction had been equal opportunity. Not one of us bore the blame more than the other. But he was right. I'd wanted him. From the moment I discovered he'd attend, I schemed to be in his company.

I should've listened to what he had to say. I should've been honest about how much I liked him. Before we spent time together, I'd had a crush on him. Afterward, I fell a little in love with him, and nothing could stop me from having sex with him.

My captor crouched in front of me, snatched the gag away, and swiped at my wet cheeks. He held a finger up. Red tears? My brows snapped together. Then, I remembered. Someone hitting me. Blood running down my face. Falling unconscious.

"I'm Dutch, Effie."

My eyes flared in surprise that he knew my name. I still refused to speak.

He smirked, leaned forward, and pressed his lips against mine. I turned my head. Struggling in protest wasn't an option. I was bound too tightly. Rough fingers sank into my cheeks and forced my head toward him.

"Kiss me like you kissed Pretty Boy outside the club," he snarled.

My mind whirled. Before I unpacked those words, Dutch slammed his mouth against mine. The kiss was harsh, but at least he didn't have bad breath. His grip on my face tightened.

"Respond to me."

I couldn't imagine that. Nor could I imagine a sexual assault or a brutal death. But I wasn't stupid. I needed to give to get. If I humanized him, perhaps he'd see me as a person rather than an object to be used, abused, and discarded.

His mouth on mine was just as brutal as the first time. Pretending he was Slice helped me endure. I even ignored the pain.

Dutch tore his lips away and stood. His erection pressed against his pants. For the first time, I noticed his cut. The denim had a bunch of patches and emblems. Until he turned, I couldn't know his club affiliation.

My stomach growled. Suddenly, my bladder felt overwhelmingly full.

"Do you know why you're here?"

I glowered at him.

His hand struck out, as fast as a cobra's strike, and landed on my jaw. My head snapped back, and blood leaked from my injured nose, sliding over my lips.

He leaned in. "Let's try this again. Why are you here, Effie?"

I hated my sniffle. My fresh tears left me feeling like a scared little girl. I was terrified, but this asshole didn't have to know it.

He struck me again. This time, stars danced behind my eyelids.

"You don't want to talk?" His fingers went to his belt. "I have another use for your fucking mouth."

Dutch had asked me about my kiss with Slice, so I knew why I was there. "This has something to do with Slice," I croaked. "Pr-pretty Boy."

Not answering, he finished unbuckling his belt and opening his fly. He shoved his hand into his underwear and—

"Yo, Dutch!"

He gave me an ugly look and stepped back, his hands falling to his side. "In here, Rusty."

Metal scraped against metal, then a door opened, and four guys swaggered in, all in denim cuts. One carried filled cup holders, and another had two pastry boxes.

My stomach growled again.

"Took long enough," Dutch sneered to the two men who carried the grub. "I'm fucking starving."

"Sorry, Dutch," a massive man with brown hair and a thick beard said. "We got a glimpse of a Death Dweller and had to lay low. Don't want beef with those motherfuckers."

Dutch grunted. Opening a box, he grabbed two donuts and tore into both at the same time. He chewed loudly, his smacking lips echoing around me and increasing my hunger. Once he finished, he grabbed two more and looked at the guy with the cupholders. "Got my cappuccino?"

"Got two for you, Dutch." He shifted his weight and squirmed like a school kid facing a reprimand. "Seeing as how we took so long and all."

One of the men whose hands were free rushed forward and picked up a cup, then held it out to Dutch. He scarfed the two donuts in his hand, grabbed the cup, and gulped, then grabbed two more donuts and polished them off.

Unfortunately, he remembered me. He crouched in front of me again, leaned in, and belched in my fucking face. I remained stoic.

"Did Pretty Boy make you come?"

How was I supposed to answer that? If I didn't respond, I had no doubt he'd shove his dick in my mouth.

"We're nothing to each other, Dutch," I said quietly.

"Bullshit, bitch," he responded. "Every time you posted pictures of that so-called event, that motherfucker was staring at you."

That explained how he knew my name and my location.

"Why don't we tag-team her?" Brown Beard said. "We'll see if he fucked her. Pretty Boy would've busted that pussy wide open."

My hunger and need to pee couldn't compare to my mortification. "I don't know what's going on between you and Slice," I said, too tired to care that my voice trembled. "But we just had a fling. He won't care that you took me. I'm innocent." I searched my brain for the right word. "A c-civilian. I'm not part of his world. I wanted a night with a biker, and he gave it to me."

Dutch stared at me.

"If anything happens to me, won't that bring more heat down on you because I don't belong to your world? Let me go and I swear I'll never mention this to anyone. Even law enforcement."

Fifty-fifty I spoke the truth. But I needed safety to think clearly. If my kidnapping was because of Slice, and, if the cops got involved, he'd be implicated, too. Whether I was his or not, I was taken *because* of him, an egregious affront in the biker world. Dead or alive, I would be avenged. No matter what I claimed.

Brown Beard turned. Satan's Sinners MC caught my attention. Dutch. Satan's Sinners. Striker and Slice discussed them the other night. I'd seen his photo and called him a scrotum.

I was in deep shit.

My stomach growled again. If I didn't use a bathroom soon, I'd wet myself.

"I need a bathroom," I said in a small voice. My mouth felt dry and cottony. I licked my cracked lips. "And some water." My stomach growled again. "And a donut."

Brown Beard shoved a whole donut in his mouth. "You have a lot of demands, slut," he said once he swallowed enough food to be understood.

"She sure does, Rusty," Dutch said, unamused. He began pacing. "Here's the thing, Effie. I'm not a man who does anything without payment. Quid pro quo. I'm especially not a motherfucker who'll be swayed by the pretty face on a bitch who fucked an asshole who stole my club's goddamn drugs. Riker brought his ass to Jackson with Goose and Drifter, then fucking refused to pay us and hand over Pretty Boy."

"We wasn't taking one without the other," Rusty volunteered, not caring if I knew any of those people. "Riker brought a thousand bands of hundreds, offered us a small cut of the profits, and flatly refused *our* terms. If he ain't wanted us to kill Pretty Boy, he could've just sent us his head and we would've called it even."

At the images the words provoked, I dry heaved.

Dutch circled me, a shark ready to pounce. "Here's the fucking deal, Effie. Red Rum has one chance for an exchange. You for Pretty Boy. We're making a video, you and me, and I'm going to send it to them with my terms. If it's one minute past the time and the terms haven't been met, I'm fucking you and sending your head to him."

He kneeled in front of me, ignoring my trembles. It didn't occur to me what he was doing until he lifted one of my boots and threw it aside, then did the same with the other. He snatched off my socks and flung them over his shoulder.

"Rusty?"

"What up, Dutch?"

"Bring as many cases as those empty bottles from the storeroom and break them. Strewn the path between here and the bathroom."

Rusty scratched his beard. "Should I make a glass path between here and the entrance, too?"

Dutch nodded.

"I have to go really bad," I whined, all my pride out the window. "I promise I'll behave."

Scowling, Dutch cut the ties around my ankles. The sudden rush of blood after the restricted flow burned my veins. He slid a finger underneath the rope tied around my body and brushed my breast, then shoved the knife into the tiny tunnel he created. I remained frozen, fearing the blade would sink into me. It didn't. Instead, the rope loosened. A couple more cuts and he stood, then yanked it away. Behind me, he made quick work of the rope around my wrists. Finally unbound, my entire body sagged, overcome with sensations zipping through me. My head whirled.

Sinking his hands into my hair, he dragged me to my feet, stared into my eyes, and cut away my shirt and bra. Automatically, my arms flew up to cover my exposed breasts. He forced them to my sides.

"Listen, you little bitch," he snarled, wrapping a big hand around my breast and squeezing painfully. "Any funny business and I will strip you to your bare ass, then discover firsthand how tight it is. You get a sip of water, but no food. When you come back, I tie you up again."

"Please don't tie me up again. My breasts are out. I have no shoes. My head is spinning and I don't know my location. I won't do anything."

He glared at me, then shoved me toward Rusty. "We'll make the video when you return. Pray Pretty Boy values you enough to bring his ass here because the clock starts ticking the moment I press send."

SLICE

"I don't know, Lennon," Daria sobbed. "I'm not sure how long she was gone before we realized it."

A dull ache settled into my gut as Daria's tears resounded throughout the silent clubhouse. Dad and Drifter were there when we arrived. Ophelia drove Daria in her car. I took the lead and Cash brought up the rear. Striker wasn't happy with me involving his club, but at Riker's orders, he allowed us to enter. Word of Effie's kidnapping had already spread throughout the membership, so when we arrived, the subdued mood reflected my feelings perfectly.

Hopelessness. Doom. Dread, especially when Cash announced he'd received a message that Effie's phone was dead. Their private investigator couldn't track her with the resources he had. Our only hope was Stretch's ability to ping the towers of her last known location. If they hadn't moved her or separated her from her phone, they'd find her that way. I couldn't imagine how, even if Red Rum possessed equipment to track phones. Austin was a big city, the capital of Texas, a vibrant active place with any number of spots to hold Effie.

"I'll call the cops myself, Daria!" Lennon's voice blared through my tortured thoughts.

"Lenny, please," Daria cried. "Don't. You'll put her at risk. This is a club matter and—"

"Daria, love, I understand you want to protect Slice, but *he* didn't protect our daughter! They don't have the resources."

Riker had the resources. *Striker* did not. Furthermore, Riker would avenge Effie as a matter of principle. He just wouldn't send anyone to save her. It was one of the few times I resented the structure of Red Rum.

"Slice, if you're listening," Lennon called, "I'm shocked and disappointed in you. Had I known you were a criminal, I wouldn't have allowed you near my wife and I especially wouldn't have let Effie within an inch of you."

"Lennon, just come to the clubhouse." Daria barely pushed the words out. She was crying so much, my anger toward her dissolved and I felt sorry for her. "We'll figure it out then. Please, I'm begging you don't do anything until then. Please, don't risk my baby. Please."

"Your baby, huh, Daria?" Lennon barked.

Across the room from me Daria sat at the bar and leaned her phone against a bottle of water, which didn't allow me to see Lennon's face. I moved restlessly in a chair at a table with Striker, Dad, Drifter, Desmond, Cash, and Dolph. We'd thrown ideas back and forth. I wanted to tear Austin apart to find Effie. Or wait until they contacted me again, hoped a number showed up so I could text back, and then offer her in exchange for me.

Cash added little to the conversation. He looked bored. Red Rum wasn't on the scale of the Death Dwellers by any means. Riker's chapter—our mother chapter—made the most money, which explained why they had the best resources. I didn't know why Cash and Stretch had come. So far, they'd offered a load of bullshit and no action. About an hour ago, we got word that Stretch was in Houston. Not long after, a motherfucker arrived with an enormous duffle bag for Cash, then nodded to us and left.

"No, that's not true!" Daria cried.

What the fuck had I missed?

"It is, Daria. You don't see me as Effie's father."

"I swear I didn't mean it like that, Lennon," Daria said hoarsely. "A girl couldn't ask for a better daddy than you. Effie adores you."

"And I know what's best for her, love." His voice had gentled. "We're calling in the cops."

Lifting a brow at me, Cash folded his arms. I didn't know what to say. I was on the verge of crashing out. Striker wanted the Death Dwellers to assist. Less collateral damage for his chapter, though I was *his* club member not *theirs.*

Striker got away with such fuckery because blood was thicker than water, and Riker allowed his brother the leeway he'd never afford anyone else. They didn't want me going off on my own, half-cocked. No, Riker ordered me to stand down and Striker and Dad agreed. They didn't care that Effie was a defenseless woman.

Ophelia plucked Daria's phone up and smiled at the asshole on the screen. "Hi, Lennon. I'm Ophelia Donovan. Daria is quite distressed right now."

"As if I'm not," Lennon responded.

"I know," Ophelia soothed. "But I'm asking on behalf of Daria and Effie to please just do as your wife suggests. I understand you want to call in the cops. You can't."

"I don't know who you are, Ophelia, and I don't care. I'm not listening to a biker slut who is tainting my wife and daughter just by breathing."

Growling, Cash jumped to his feet, stalked to Ophelia, and snatched the phone. "Motherfucker, this is how this is going. Some of my brothers will arrive at your house shortly. If you call the cops at any time from now to the end of eternity, they will find fucking pieces of you."

"Joke's on you, sir," Lennon said with indignation.

I agreed. More hyperbolic bullshit from Cash's arrogant ass. No fucking way would he know what Lennon did, now or later.

Lennon snorted. "We have security cameras. You'll be identified."

"*Not*. They'd have to see the fucking footage," Cash retorted. A doorbell rang. "That should be Saw and Ziggy now. My patience is gone. My nerves are raw and I'm highly fucking insulted on behalf of my woman. Don't fucking piss me off any further."

Lennon screamed. "How the fuck did you get in—" His words abruptly cut off and he gasped.

The distinctive sound of a body thudding to the ground came through the line.

"We got him, Cash," a new voice said.

They...*what?*

"How do you want us to deliver him?"

"Alive," Cash said grudgingly. "His woman wants him in one piece. Blindfold him and throw him in the back of the van. I suggest you gag his ass so you're not tempted to fuck him up when he comes to, Saw."

Saw snickered. "Got it, brother."

"Watch your ass," Cash said. "Satan's Sinner motherfuckers are crawling. I would hate to have to blow them the fuck out of existence so far from home."

"Damn, this motherfucker is heavy," another new voice grunted.

"Stop whining like a pussy, Ziggy," Cash said around laughter. He gave them the address of the Austin club. "I'll text you directions from my phone."

"You got it, brother."

My phone alerted me to an incoming message. Unlike the first two messages, this one revealed digits, complete with a '601' area code. A Jackson, Mississippi number.

The multimedia message took a moment to load. When it did, I opened it immediately and almost dropped to my knees.

Dutch stood behind Effie. She was topless, her nose and cheeks were swollen, bloodied, and bruised.

"Speak, Effie," Dutch ordered.

"Effie!" Daria cried, rousing from her near stupor.

Cash barreled over with Daria and Ophelia hot on his heels. They crowded behind me before I could warn Daria away or tell Cash not to look.

"What have they done to her?" Daria cried.

Dutch slapped Effie and she reeled back. He grabbed a handful of hair and put a knife to her throat. "Talk."

Tears brimmed in her eyes, but she glared at him. I felt sick to my fucking stomach. Any moment, I expected Dutch to slit her throat.

"Come on, baby," I said, shocked at how my own voice trembled. "Don't be stubborn, Effie."

Dutch pressed the knife into her skin. Daria screamed and fainted, so I paused the video. Ophelia held her until Dolph stood and lifted her into his arms, carrying her away. He walked out of the clubhouse with her. I assumed to bring her around the corner to Prissy's place.

I pressed play and resumed the video.

"One more fucking chance, you stubborn little cunt," Dutch roared. "Speak or die."

"Slice," Effie said, and her little sob broke my fucking heart. "I will never regret our time together. I only wish we had longer and I'm so sorry I wasn't willing to hear you out. I never believed in love. The only pure and genuine love I saw was between my parents, but I fell in love with you over the course of the last eighteen months during our conversations. I just didn't realize it until we were in each other's company. I love you. I know you don't feel the same and that's okay. Tell Mom I love her and I'm so sorry our last interaction ended the way it did. I love her so much. I love her, Dad, Heath, and Cassie." She swiped at her tears. "I still think Chad's a fucking asshole but tell her I wish her all the happiness in the world."

She went silent.

"Say the rest, Effie," Dutch ordered.

"Fuck you."

"Hold my phone, Rusty."

I knew Rusty. He had a bushy beard and an empty head. Effie crumpled at the blow to her midsection. Dutch yanked her to her feet and shoved her closer to the camera.

He wrapped an arm around her neck and began fondling her tit. "You want this bitch back alive, *Pretty Boy*? You have twenty-four hours to get to Jackson and turn yourself in. Otherwise, we'll take her head in place of yours and consider the bounty paid."

The call ended.

"Send me that clip," Cash ordered.

I didn't move. I continued staring at the phone and the thumbnail of the video where Effie professed her love and refused to tell me to exchange my life for hers.

Ophelia attempted to take my phone, but I tightened my hold.

"Fuck!" Cash yanked it away. "Fall apart when she's back." He pressed a few buttons, then threw my phone on the table. "We need all hands on deck."

"So far, all you've done is issue orders," I snapped, unhinging. I got to my feet and kicked my chair, wishing it was Dutch. "You have a lot of fucking nerve acting as if you know what I'm feeling. No one that you love has ever been in fucking danger."

"Listen up, motherfucker—"

"I have a fucking name," I sneered, debating on ignoring everyone's orders and finding Effie. I was past the point of caring about orders and past the point of diplomacy with Cash. "And it isn't motherfucker."

"It could be motherfucking Bugs Bunny," Cash barked, unfazed by my anger. He was tall and muscular, but I wasn't a fucking runt. And, despite how well-preserved he was, he was older than me. One-on-one, I'd wipe the fucking floor with his ass. "I don't want to be here any more than you fucking want me here, but Outlaw and Goose are acquaintances and I got marching orders to assess the situation and see what the fuck was needed to *assist* Red Rum. You motherfuckers don't have the technology. You don't have space. You don't have fire power, so shut the fuck up, sit the fuck down, and let me do my goddamn job so I can get back to Hortensia and see my fucking children."

I couldn't believe he'd procreated and populated the world with more little hims. Fucking asshole.

Cash stalked to the wall behind our table and hefted the duffle bag that had sat forgotten since it was delivered.

Glaring at me, he removed his guns at his sides, then the shoulder holster. He stripped down to his bulletproof vest and underwear, and replaced his jeans, white T-shirt, and cut with the name 'Cash' to an all-black outfit and a cut with 'Ghost.' He strapped up again and grabbed another handgun from the bag and two skinning knives.

Somehow, I didn't allow my mouth to fall open. Yeah, we'd opened this can of worms when I was ordered to steal the drugs. And, yeah, that was a fucking capital offense to *intercept* another club's merchandise. And, yeah, Cash was right—I almost strangled on that admission—about what we did and didn't have.

But fuck me sideways, I'd never seen as much hardware.

"Striker, Goose?" he grouched, grabbing a Barrett rifle from the bag and laying it across the chair. "I told Outlaw the situation. He understands your position and in solidarity wants you two to split the guns and ammo left in this duffle between your two clubs."

Striker spat on the floor. "Keep those fucking guns. My chapter's not into all that. We're fine with our nines and thirty-eights."

Desmond and Dolph shifted and pressed their lips together. Their yearning gazes called Striker a fucking liar, but they remained silent, staring at Cash's assault rifle.

"*Goose,*" Cash gritted. Throwing shade with that one word and a side-eye was a fucking art. "There are two more Barretts in the duffle. I'll have someone disassemble them for your easy transport. They're MRADS." He nodded to his. "Not the M107 like mine."

"Outlaw told me you were a sniper in the military," Dad said.

Cash nodded. "I was. Now, I'm the club's sniper and bomb tech."

A few whistles went up. I hated my own admiration. Cash was an arrogant fuckhead.

Cash pointed to the bag. "Riker is already aware of the munitions."

"Exactly my fucking point!" Striker blared. "Munitions? That has to do with fucking combat! A combat package or some shit."

Dad snatched the toothpick out of his mouth and pointed it at Striker. "Didn't I just confirm the motherfucker is former military? Makes sense he'd use that term, fuckhead."

Folding his arms, Striker glowered but shut the fuck up.

Cash glanced at his watch, then his phone. As if on cue, it rang. "Talk to me," he answered.

"The phone that sent the video pinged from a tower near a warehouse close to the Colorado River," Stretch said, on speakerphone. "It's the same tower Effie's phone pinged from before we lost the signal."

"What's the address of her location?" Cash demanded, a vital piece of information I wanted badly.

"We're searching for cameras around where the phones pinged, Cash," Stretch answered. "I can send a general location, but you don't want to give us away by searching the area."

"I hate it when you're right."

Stretch laughed. "Deal with it, fuckhead. Fair warning, Outlaw isn't happy. He didn't know we took Fee."

"I'll call him," Ophelia promised.

"He said I should've taken you with me, babe. Sent you to Josh if you didn't want to come to the club."

"I had to see to Daria. I'll make him see reason."

"Call Meggie," Stretch said. "She'll calm him down. Tell her that her favorite sister-in-law wanted to meet her favorite author and we couldn't deny her."

Ophelia giggled. "You're so silly. I'll talk to her so she can calm my brother down and remind him of how crazy with worry he was when she was kidnapped, and also when I was stabbed."

That startled me.

"Don't bring that up, Ophelia," Stretch said quietly.

"Yeah, don't," Cash added flatly. "I'll regret Noah's easy fucking death for the rest of my fucking life."

"At least you got to participate," Stretch complained.

"Are you two fucking insane?" Despite the snickers amongst us, Ophelia sounded appalled. "Arguing over, er...over..."

"Fucking a motherfucker up for fucking with you?" Cash supplied.

"Yep," she said with a sniff.

"I only beheaded him. Johnnie would've cut little chunks out of him."

Ophelia blanched. "You *what*?"

"Shut the fuck up, Fee. That motherfucker left you for dead." Cash raised his hands. "It's done. His pieces were dropped into acid, thrown in the water, and turned to compost over a decade ago."

"Goddamn," I breathed.

"Ignore Cash the Grouch, Fee," Stretch soothed. "It's all good, babe."

"Get back to work, Stretch." Cash glared from Ophelia to the phone's screen. "This walk down memory lane serves no purpose. It especially isn't getting Effie back. Find her. You have three fucking hours. I want this over, Effie safe, and us on the road in the next twelve."

"Josh is on standby with the plane if we need medical facilities for anyone," Stretch said, unperturbed by Cash's orders.

A plane? The club had a fucking airplane? That left me fucking reeling. Striker didn't even have *tracking* equipment.

"Outlaw also wants to know if he should send Diesel?" Stretch went on, the question clear in his voice.

"For legal matters or executions?" Cash asked.

"Both, I assume," Stretch responded. "Diesel will see the latter as a bonus. Outlaw mentioned defense counsel, however."

"Tell him to keep Diesel on standby, too," Cash instructed, took the phone off speaker, and put it to his ear.

The more I heard, the more my adrenaline pumped. Ideas on how to get Dad's chapter of Red Rum to where the Dwellers were, ran through my head. Once we saved Effie.

"Get it done, Stretch," Cash barked and disconnected. "Call your brother in twenty minutes, Fee. Slice, come with me. Striker, get as many members here as possible—"

"We're all here, Cash," Striker inserted with resentment.

Cash glanced from man to man and scrubbed a hand over his face. "Get all the chicks affiliated with your club here now."

"We need to go on lockdown?" Dad asked.

Striker stiffened and shook his head. "Riker hasn't approved that."

"Well, your brother isn't here," Drifter said. "We are. I'll call Riker and fill him in. But Dad's right. We're in danger. We don't know where the rest of Dutch's club members are."

"He's only sent out for special assignments," Striker insisted. "He has four other motherfuckers in his crew."

"Here's the fucking deal," Cash said. "Order a fucking temporary lockdown. I'm not risking Ophelia. I understand Effie is in danger, but I'll walk out that fucking door and take my woman with me unless you guarantee her safety."

Dad didn't have jurisdiction over another man's club, but he whispered to Striker.

The motherfucker finally nodded. "Fine."

"Then let's get this show on the road, kiddies," Cash said.

Effie

Someone was on top of me.

Full awareness took a moment to seep into my foggy brain. I'd lost track of time and place. After my video concluded, Dutch punched me for disobeying him and then jabbed me with another needle. Now, I'd slept off whatever the hell they gave me. Awakening to more danger sent adrenaline pumping through my veins.

I barely caught my breath because of the heaviness of the man over me. The stench of alcohol filled my nose and the swears reaching my ears let me know he was having some problems. Thankfully, my panties were still on, and between my legs didn't feel abused.

He forced my legs apart; I screamed, not that it would do any good. Lashing out, I punched blindly. It was dark and I was on the cold concrete, but my punch landed and my knuckles stung.

Suddenly, I was free and I rolled to my side. Before I hopped to my feet, he seized me again.

"Lights! Lights!" he called. "Put the fucking lights on."

"Don't take too long, Buck," Rusty responded, though I couldn't see him. "I don't want Dutch to hand me my fucking ass because of *your* horny ass."

The overhead lights flicked on, and I heard footsteps departing.

"Behave," Buck slurred. "Dutch isn't here. I want some pussy from you before he gets back. For now, you're his leverage."

"No, no, no!" I squirmed and tried to upend him, but he didn't budge.

He slapped my face, not as hard as Dutch. Because of the abuse I'd endured, the lick was still painful.

"Behave," Buck ordered again. "I don't want to kick your fucking skull in because you piss me off. Dutch won't be too pleased."

I made a conscious effort to keep my breathing slow and steady, even when he straddled me again. With the light on, I could now examine the bastard on top of me. He was old enough to be my father, with thinning hair and a messy beard sprinkled with gray. He went back to struggling with his belt, too immersed in his task to realize I was watching him, searching for an opportunity to escape, but careful not to give myself away. Older or not, he was still a man who was larger than me, one with foul intent. I wouldn't blindly hit again. I'd bide my time and wait; the element of surprise would be my best friend.

"Stupid fucking thing," he grumbled when he finally got the belt unbuckled.

My stomach dropped. He pawed at my tits, and it took everything in me not to flinch.

"Pretty little cunt, aren't you?" he breathed, his rancid breath washing over my face.

The C-word was one of the most offensive in the English language. It was degrading and belittling. If I allowed it to torture me now, I'd never save myself.

He tossed the belt aside, parting my legs. When his hands touched my panties, I couldn't remain passive. With speed I didn't know I possessed, I grabbed the belt and swung, socking him in the eye with the buckle. Luck was on my side because the prong jammed into his eye socket.

"Fucking bitch!" he screamed, yanking the prong out and clutching his bleeding injury. "You're fucking dead, you hear me?"

If he didn't shut up, I definitely would be. The arrival of backup would cut my chances of survival. As it was, I knew Rusty was lurking. Thankfully, the building I was in was large and cluttered, so there was a chance *only* Rusty heard the commotion.

Buck reached for me. I kicked at his hand, scurrying back. My mind scrambled to formulate a plan. Attacking him wasn't the smartest move, but I wouldn't allow myself to be defiled. That would be a mental scar that'd never heal.

I wasn't a survivalist. I was a sheltered middle-class girl raised in suburbia, who'd never known what it was to struggle, let alone fight for my life. And yet, as my instincts took over, I managed to inflict another injury on him. This time, I scratched his face. He recoiled, and I put more distance between us.

"I'm going to gut you, you little whore," he hissed, his hand closing around my ankle just as I managed to stand.

He sent me crashing to the floor and I cried out. Jumping on top of me again, he pinned my wrists above my head.

"Get the fuck off me!" I screeched, panic like I'd never felt before consuming me.

A backhand rewarded my words. My head snapped to the side, dots appearing in my vision as the taste of blood filled my mouth.

"Shut the fuck up," he ordered, his hand going to his fly. "I'm going to enjoy breaking you."

No, no, fucking no.

My body pinned under his, my hands disabled, made my situation bleak. The sound of his fly unzipping taunted me. His hands returned to my panties. My mind shut off, my instincts again kicking in. This time, they drew inspiration from a popular zombie show. Before I processed my actions, my teeth sank into the guy's jugular. I nearly gagged as blood filled my mouth. His scream echoed in my ears, but I didn't stop. I bit down harder, sank deeper into the vein, and jerked my head back, tearing his throat open.

Time stopped as he went limp. Just like that, the attack ended. As my adrenaline faded, realization set in. I killed someone. A sob escaped; the entire situation overwhelmed me. I wanted to curl up and hide, but that wasn't an option.

Oddly, I felt no guilt or moral dilemma over taking a man's life. It was me or him, and I still wasn't out of the woods. I'd freak out when I was safe and sound.

Thankfully, he'd fallen on the side of me. Otherwise, I wouldn't have been able to move his deadweight. Not wanting to alert Rusty, I held in another sob and turned in a circle, searching for an exit.

Glass was strewn everywhere. True to his word, Dutch must've had Rusty break the bottles to hinder me from attempting escape. As if the clutter wasn't hindrance enough. I'd take my chances and hope a door to freedom stood in the opposite direction from where I'd heard Rusty's voice.

SLICE

Standing outside the clubhouse as the first rays of sun broke through the darkness of dawn, I'd never felt more lost and alone. Even when I watched my mother breathe her last, leaving Dad, Drifter, and me heartbroken, I didn't feel such gut-wrenching pain. It hadn't come with guilt and hopelessness. Only plain damn grief and heartache.

Mom's death hadn't been easy. Asthma claimed her. But it hadn't been brutal either. Dutch would torture and abuse Effie. If Cash hadn't brought me outside and ordered me to hand him my fucking keys, I would be almost to Jackson by now.

"Floyd?"

Shoving my hands in my pockets, I glanced over my shoulder at the sound of Drifter's voice. My twin hadn't called me by my name since I'd ordered him to stop calling me 'Pretty Boy Floyd' when I was sixteen. Riker had shortened it to 'Pretty Boy'.

It didn't matter. Drifter backed up Cash. They were both on my shit list. My brother couldn't soften me with familiarity.

"I know you're angry, brother, but you're not thinking logically. You would've gotten to Jackson, sacrificed yourself, and she'd still end up dead."

My nostrils flared. I didn't know how I'd ever make it up to Effie if she survived. Maybe, she wouldn't even want me to.

"You love her. Love makes a man crazy."

I had said I loved her, hadn't I? At least in so many words.

"You two boys want a cigarette?"

Cash held his freshly opened pack between us. I hadn't heard the door open. Then again, I was lost in my own misery.

Drifter accepted Cash's offer. "Come on, Pretty Boy Floyd. It'll take the edge off."

Amusement danced in Cash's blue eyes. He took a drag on his cigarette, then released the smoke through his mouth and nose. "Now I understand."

Snatching a cigarette and lighting it, I took a drag. "Shocking that you understand anything. Assholes rarely do."

Cash smirked. "I'm a very self-aware asshole, so fuck you. It wasn't the insult you thought it would be."

"What do you understand?" I grumbled.

"Why the fuck you're shaming the fucking brotherhood with a name like Pretty Boy and *modeling*," Cash retorted. He nodded to Drifter. "You have the same face but not as much vanity."

"My mother got both of us into modeling," Drifter said. "I hated it. Pretty Boy took to it like a fish to water. My last gig was as an eight-year-old. Floyd did it until he was twelve or thirteen."

Cash dragged on his cigarette. "Pretty Boy's a shitty road name, by the way."

"It was a childhood nickname that carried over to my biker life," I said, following Cash and Drifter's lead and enjoying my smoke. "I want to change it to Slice. Maybe, I'll use you as an example and appeal to Riker to use both. Haven't met too many motherfuckers with two road names."

"Don't have two. My name is Cash. Ghost is my road name. I use it less and less these days. I've become a steward of peace."

Whatever that meant. I didn't care to find out.

A white van with blacked-out windows swerved to a stop feet away from us. The passenger and driver's side doors opened and two motherfuckers jumped out. The driver headed to Cash, while the passenger stalked to the back, allowing me a glimpse of the Death Dweller emblem.

"Problems, Saw?" Cash drawled as the driver reached us.

He bumped fists with Cash. "I started to dump that motherfucker on the side of the road, Cash," Saw answered. "Ziggy was a word away from icing him. He wouldn't shut the fuck up."

"That's why I suggested the gag, fuckhead."

Saw grunted.

"I can't see without my glasses!"

Immediately, I recognized Lennon's voice. Apparently, he still wouldn't shut the fuck up. Ziggy marched Daria's husband into view. A ginger with a buzz cut wasn't a bad thing, but the asshole looked as if he never got any sun.

A cotton ball had more color.

Sidling a glare at Lennon as he halted next to him, Saw dug into his pocket and came up with a pair of glasses. "Here, motherfucker."

Lacking the ability to see his abductors should've been counted as a win. If he couldn't identify us, we wouldn't have to pluck out his fucking eyes.

Once Lennon perched his glasses on his nose, he went from nerd to pasty monstrosity. His furious hazel gaze found me. "You!"

Cash folded his arms. "Your son-in-law's been through enough, Lenny Boy."

Lennon's throat worked. He stared at Cash, turned to me, then looked at Cash again. "My...are you...my *what*?" he finally spluttered, his eyes bulging.

Saw and Ziggy sniggered. I couldn't deny how Lenny's shock and panic amused me. Cash was such a messy motherfucker.

"Only a matter of time before Slice puts a ring on it." Cash flicked his cigarette away. "Might as well get used to it."

"Over my dead body," Lennon spat. He looked at me again, his eyes burning with dislike and disgust.

"Your demise can happily be arranged," Cash said calmly. "But I think Daria would be a little broken up over your death."

"You're joking," Lennon said, although he'd lost some of his contempt. "All the biker killers in Daria's books are so named. Savage. Butcher. Executioner. Knife. Sword. Poison. Garrot. Prisoner."

"Prisoner?" Drifter and Saw echoed in outrage.

"We have Mortician," Cash supplied.

Lennon frowned. "You've hired a funeral home to seek revenge on your behalf?"

"Nope. Mort's our enforcer. Although we do have a funeral home. Makes things easier. Especially disposal. Little evidence means less questions."

"You don't look like the way Daria describes her killers," Lennon said. He nodded to Cash's cut. "You don't even have a killer's name. Ghost is generic."

"Ghost was earned. I kill enemies without ever being seen. Did it for my country and I do it for my club. As for what Daria writes, it's fiction and her names are a fucking travesty. Not even actual prisoners want to be called *Prisoner*."

Lennon frowned.

"But," Cash growled, "this situation isn't a made-up drama. Your daughter is in real danger with real bad men. Get your fucking head out of your cockhole, man the fuck up, and support your wife."

"That's why I'm here." Lennon drew himself up. "In case you didn't realize that."

"You're here because you didn't have a fucking choice, asshole," Cash said.

Enjoying myself, I flicked my smoke away and grinned.

"Supporting your wife means cooperating and shutting the fuck up unless I need something from you," Cash continued. "It definitely doesn't mean calling in the fucking badges. Because, motherfucker, if you do, that'll risk my president's freedom, too. And that means he'd be taken away from his wife, whom he worships. Fuck with her, you fuck with him, and that's the quickest fucking way to get yourself killed. So I'll save him the goddamn headache—he's also my common law brother-in-law—and kill you myself."

Swallowing, Lennon looked at me with expectation. Did he really expect me to step in after he'd just shit all over me? I shrugged.

"No cops," Lennon said finally. "Where's Daria?"

Cash looked at me, punting the decision to allow Lennon in the club in my court. The motherfucker had been running the fucking show for hours. But I appreciated the gesture.

"She's inside," I said. "Prissy brought her here a couple of hours ago when she brought us coffee and donuts." I stepped aside so he could pass.

"That is what Sloane would call a certified asshole," Cash chortled once Lennon disappeared inside.

Ziggy and Saw snickered.

"How is our rock star?" Saw asked. "My old lady still sucks me off in appreciation of you introducing her to the members of Phoenix Rising."

My eyes widened. "Wait, you were telling the truth?"

"Unfortunately," Cash grumbled.

"Fuck off, Cash," Ziggy said. "You know you like that motherfucker."

Cash grinned. I understood why Lennon found it hard to believe he was a killer. Cash was handsome and clean-cut, even in his colors. He was surly but rather charming.

"I admit to nothing, fuckhead," he said. He turned to me. "By the way, these are my brothers. Saw and Ziggy. Both from our Corpus Christi chapter. This is...uh, Slice."

"Who are you?" Saw asked my brother. "Portion?"

"Segment?" Ziggy supplied. "Half? Cake? Pie? Pizza?"

"All right, fuckheads," Cash said, joining in the laughter. "That's his twin. Drifter."

Another concession. Formal introductions.

Once we all bumped fists, Cash brought Saw and Ziggy up to speed on the video and that last call with Stretch. It was well past Cash's allotted three hours and there'd not been another update. I'm not sure what I would've done had I remained alone outside.

But the distraction only lasted so long. The lull in conversation brought my helplessness and desperation back. I just wanted to know Effie was alive. I wanted to look into her eyes again and tell her...tell her that I loved her.

"Hold your shit together, Slice," Cash said.

"Give me my fucking keys so I can search for her myself."

In the distance, the unmistakable sound of Harleys broke the stillness of the morning.

"No. I'll give you the keys when it's time to leave," Cash said. "You'll get you and her killed. You want a chance at your happily-ever-after with babies and puppy dogs, you're doing this my way."

"There'll be no HEA for her and me. I can't live a double life. I'll always be a biker. Riker will send me on missions that endanger me. If we're together, she's in danger, too."

"Then Riker must want you dead," Cash said.

Drifter stiffened. "That's *my* Prez."

"Don't give a fuck. Just like Slice can be Bugs Bunny for all I care, Riker could be your little old granny. Why the fuck would he order you to steal another club's drugs without the resources to fix that shit when it goes sideways? Theft of that magnitude takes months of fucking planning and strategizing so your identity will remain unknown, you stupid motherfucker."

"I didn't steal! I intercepted."

"No, you fucked up," Cash barked. "Call it what the fuck it is."

"Riker wanted the drugs for an infusion of money," Drifter said. "It was to benefit our entire organization."

"It's baby steps, fuckhead. Two hundred fifty grand worth of narcotics with a fucking street value ten times that amount? All you motherfuckers are insane."

Saw and Ziggy nodded in agreement.

The roar of bikes drowned out any more conversation. Long before I became a biker, I loved motorcycles. Nothing like such a powerful machine vibrating between my thighs as I ate up the miles. And this show of force was the type of drama Drifter and I imagined when we'd first joined Red Rum.

Stretch dismounted from his bike, walked up to us, and greeted Saw and Ziggy. Once he introduced himself to Drifter, he looked at Cash.

"Well?"

"I have her location, Cash," Stretch confirmed. "It isn't far from the hotel."

So it wasn't far from the club.

"Drifter, let Striker know we're heading out," Cash said. "Ziggy, Saw, you let anything happen to Fee and I'll gut you."

"That's Outlaw's sister and John Boy's cousin," Saw said. "We don't want to disappoint any of you."

Ziggy nodded. "Yeah, we value our lives too much."

"Striker isn't coming?" I asked.

"Nope." Cash dug into his pocket. "Don't want him with me. He's casting blame for bringing attention to his quiet club. Let his quiet fucking ass stay here and help to protect Fee, Daria, and your club girls." He nodded to his brothers. "We got this."

He tossed my keys to me. I caught them on reflex.

"*Now*, motherfucker, you have your keys and we ride."

Effie

Exhaustion threatened to finish me off. I'd come so far only to face defeat. Soaking wet and in only my panties, I dropped onto the ground and heaved in a breath. Shortly, I would die. Rusty would find me. He'd make me pay for what I did to Buck. Even if I survived his retribution, I wouldn't be as lucky with Dutch.

My escape was for nothing. I wish I'd just submitted to that brute. Fight or flight kicked in and I followed my gut reaction. He might have left me so brutalized, my emotional scars wouldn't have ever healed and I would've wished he'd killed me. I wouldn't ever find out. He was dead.

I had killed *him*.

Swallowing, I swiped my hands across my lips, the metallic taste of blood heavy in my mouth. Tears pooled in my eyes and I dry heaved. I'd had two sips of water during my captivity and no food. Now that the danger was over, my adrenaline dipped and weakness, fatigue, and hunger set in.

After sprinting to the back of the building, I'd found an open window and climbed through it. I rejoiced. Luck had finally caught up to me. Unfortunately, my celebration was premature. Once I swung myself over the sill and dropped the short distance to the ground, I ran into another barrier. A huge fence separated me and freedom. Just beyond it, a walkway ran seemingly into infinity, since it was dark and I couldn't see more than a few feet.

Undeterred, I searched the fence for a gate or any opening. Voilà, a swath of chain link torn away. I'd sprinted through it. Not realizing how close water ran alongside the walkway, I'd tumbled in. Somehow, I managed to grab onto brambles and climb out. A few seconds later, glass pierced the sole of my left foot. I barely felt the pain, so I took a moment to pull the shard out, though walking proved painful. I hadn't gotten the entire piece out of my foot. Uncertain of my whereabouts, cold and in pain, I ended up right back where I began. On the warehouse grounds.

The water had washed away Buck's blood but left me drenched. I'd just tucked myself into a corner of the building when a beam of light shone from the window I'd jumped from.

"Fuck!" Rusty snarled. "That cunt killed my brother."

"Yep. Buck's dead. *We're* alive and Dutch will have our asses for letting her escape."

"If she escaped and fell into the water, the current probably swept that bitch away," Rusty speculated without a shred of remorse. "Fuck her. I hope a gator devours her."

I pressed my hand against my mouth to hold in my sob.

"She might still be out there. We'll look in the morning. At least, we'll tell Dutch the truth when we say we searched for her."

Rusty grunted. "Put on the alarm just in case. If that little cunt is out there, it will go off the minute she moves."

Another tense moment went by before silence fell again. Still, I didn't move, afraid it was a ruse to smoke me out.

Hours later, the sun finally rose. I hadn't slept a wink, but the chill that chased me morphed into so much heat I thought I'd burst into flames. I needed to move, but I couldn't think straight to create a decent plan. My cell phone was long gone. My exact location was unknown to me.

The sound of a motorcycle reached me, and I deflated. If I returned voluntarily, maybe Dutch would kill me quickly. I just wanted the nightmare to end.

Slice rose in my mind and I smiled, hoping he saw the video. I didn't regret my defiance. Deep down, I'd known I wouldn't make it out alive. Even if Slice complied and agreed to exchange his life for mine. Dutch was a horrible asshole. He would never have stuck to the plan.

Closing my eyes, I curled into a tighter ball, aware I lay on the ground, shivering despite how overheated I felt.

Visions of my family played in my head. My dad driving me to ballet class. Mom bustling about, teaching me to cook, then hurrying me to soccer practice where she'd write until it ended. Heath calling me 'spaghetti arms' like Johnny said to Baby in *Dirty Dancing*. Not for dancing, though. My brother was teaching me to fight.

I sniffled. Fat lot of good those lessons did.

Memories of Cass replaced Heath. Good memories, back when we were still friends and when I wasn't so judgmental of her life choices.

A hand sank into my hair and wrenched me to my feet, then slapped me to the ground.

"You little bitch," Dutch snarled, furious, grabbing my throat and jerking me up. "You killed Buck."

I didn't want to die. I was tired and scared and a bunch of things. No matter how resigned I was to my death, I wanted to live and I'd fight until my dying breath.

Dutch dangled me like a rag doll. My adrenaline spiked. I jabbed my finger into his eye as hard as I could. He screamed and dropped me. Ignoring the jolt of pain, I scrambled to my feet and kicked his cock. He sank to the ground.

I sprinted toward the break in the fence, but Rusty catapulted out of the open window and landed in front of me. I kneed his junk, too. One of the other dudes climbed from the window. Evading him, I spun and ran toward the front of the warehouse. The distance between me and the front gate was much longer, but those assholes kept swooping from that stupid window like bats on a belfry.

Screaming at the top of my lungs, I expected a bullet to tear into me at any minute. A line of motorcycles roared through the open gate and I screamed again. Dutch's club members!

I turned and—

Dutch socked me in my belly, knocking the wind from me. I dropped to the ground. He attacked immediately and kicked my back, then straddled me and wrapped his hands around my throat.

Suddenly, I was free. Turning to my side, I coughed and sputtered, gasping for air. Grunts and curses broke the silent morning. Sounds of a fight. Motorcycles rumbling.

Gathering the last of my energy, I lifted myself into a sitting position. Slice swung a machete and Dutch's head went flying.

"Slice," I mumbled. "Now, I know why."

I fainted.

SLICE

Daria and Lennon demanded medical care for Effie and expressed outrage at Cash's insistence we take her to the clubhouse. I thought he was out of his fucking mind, too. It didn't matter how many questions I faced—how much time I'd end up doing—I couldn't see a way around *not* rushing her to the ER.

But I was outnumbered. Out of my club members, only Drifter and Dad rode with us. Striker refused to allow anyone from the Austin chapter to ride at my side, though Dolph, Desmond, and Raider volunteered.

Since the Death Dwellers were on the line too and considering they'd risked their lives to assist when my brothers wouldn't, I ceded to their demands. While we searched the warehouse, Cash ordered Saw and Ziggy to bring the van used to transport Lennon. They took Effie back to the club in the van. Unfortunately, they also placed two dead men, one head, and three live Satan's Sinners in with her.

Back at the club, I rushed to the van, expecting a hysterical Effie. She remained unconscious. When I carried her in, Daria lost her shit. By now, her son and other daughter had arrived. I knew this because they looked like Lennon *and* they sat at a table with him.

Cash ignored their insistence that we call an ambulance and ordered me to lay Effie on the bar. Her injuries horrified me and I regretted killing Dutch so quickly. He deserved a slow, painful death for what he'd done to her.

I kissed Effie's cracked, bloody lips. Her bruised cheeks. Her blackened eyelids. Her swollen nose. I touched her neck, the imprint of Dutch's miserable fingers so clear on her once flawless skin. I caressed her battered belly, almost lost my shit at the purpling on her breasts. Even in her state, she shivered.

"I'm so sorry, baby," I whispered.

Cash shoved me out of the way and covered Effie with a thermal blanket. "See to her cuts, Ophelia," he ordered.

Sick to death of Cash, I pushed him. "Motherfucker," I gritted. "Keep your fucking hands to yourself."

"Shut the fuck up," he barked as Ophelia snapped on medical gloves and dug into a first aid kit.

Furious, I swiped that paltry shit away. Ophelia halted and blinked at me.

Cash lunged, but Stretch held him back.

"Stop, Cash. He's upset," he soothed.

"I don't give a fuck. That *upset* motherfucker will respect Fee."

"*Effie* needs a hospital," I snarled.

"Motherfucker, you call an ambulance and we all go to jail." Cash jerked out of Stretch's hold. "We have no contacts in Austin. We don't have a chapter here. Calm the fuck down. It's fucking handled. Josh is landing the McCall family plane shortly with help."

Saw stepped next to me. The club was silent. Even Effie's parents had quieted.

"Your woman's foot is injured. Ziggy picked out the glass on the way here and wrapped it with his T-shirt, but at least let Ophelia disinfect it."

My woman. Effie. Yeah, she was my woman. Whether she hated me after this didn't matter. In my heart, she'd always belong to me.

"We can't afford a private plane." Daria looked as broken as she sounded. "Please, let us take her. We'll say she went for a walk and didn't return. We searched for her one last time before we filed a missing person's report and found her ourselves. We won't even bring up any of your names. Just please let me help my baby."

Cash's face softened and he laid his hand between Daria's shoulder blades. "I know you're scared, Daria. I've put my mother through enough to recognize it, but I swear we will get her the best care available. If she needs more care than we can provide and we can't figure something out, we'll fly her to Hortensia. We have control over the hospital there. We don't expect payment. Outlaw is all about family. His little sister is a fan of your work and thinks Effie is great. That's all he needed to hear. What his wife, daughters, sisters, and nieces want, he gives them."

Effie groaned and began coughing. Opening her eyes, she popped into a sitting position. The blanket fell away and exposed her tits.

"Mom?" she called. "Mom? Don't be mad at me, Mom. I'm so sorry."

Daria threw her arms around her. "I'm here, baby. I'm here. I love you. I love you," she chanted.

"Where's Dad?" Effie asked as if Daria's words didn't sink in. "Mom? Are you mad at me? Where's Dad? I hope he doesn't hate me."

"I could never hate you, princess," Lennon said around a sob. "I love you."

Effie coughed again. "I'm so hot and cold. I want Cassie to read a story to me and fix her soup. Never mind," she mumbled. "I smell it. I love you, Cass."

"I love you too, Effie," Cassie said, sniffling.

"Tell Heath I fought just like he taught me. He's the best big brother ever."

Heath nodded and pressed his lips together, although Effie didn't see him. Her gaze was unfocused and she faced a different direction.

Effie swayed.

"Lay down, love," Ophelia said softly.

"Okay."

"I'm placing you on speakerphone, Mortician." Until Cash spoke, I didn't realize he'd stepped away. "Tell Fee what to do."

"Which bag Stretch grabbed?" a voice said from Cash's phone that now rested on the bar near Effie's head. "You see IV supplies? Any vials of meds and syringes?"

Ophelia looked around at what my tantrum had scattered on the bar and the floor. "Negative. I think it's just a basic kit."

"It is," Stretch said. "I thought we were only coming for recon. That's why we've scrambled to get what we need."

"She's pretty bad off, Mort," Ophelia said hesitantly.

"Fuck. Give me a few minutes," Mortician said. "Austin, right?"

"Yeah," Cash supplied.

The line disconnected.

"Slice?" Effie called and burst into tears. "Where's Slice? I tried to save him. Dutch is a liar and a motherfucker. Tell him don't go to Jackson. They'll kill him and I love him," she rambled.

"I'm here, sweetheart," I said, surprised when Daria stepped back and allowed me to take her place. I brushed my lips over Effie's, emotions swirling inside me. "Hey."

Her unfocused gaze studied me and a smile tipped up her lips. "Slice—"

"Sit her up," Ophelia said. "She's burning up. We have to bring her temperature down."

"When are we going to the airport?" I demanded, following Ophelia's instructions. Holding the blanket in place, I wrapped an arm around Effie. Once she swallowed the acetaminophen, I guided her back down. "What are we waiting for?"

"That would be me."

I glanced over my shoulder and found a man with black hair, dressed in trousers, loafers, and a button-down, smirking at Cash.

"Fucking asshole," he snapped. "I fucking told you to wear jeans, Josh."

"Which is why I wore trousers, big brother." Josh zeroed in on my cut and smiled at me. "I love fucking with him." Stepping to where I stood, he patted me on the back.

The *Addams Family Theme Song* blasted through the clubhouse. Josh lifted a brow, Stretch shook his head, and Ophelia rolled her eyes as Cash answered.

"Josh there?" Mortician asked.

Despite the serious situation, a chuckle escaped me. Fucking Cash. I didn't understand why he chose that song, but his little brain probably justified it.

"I just rolled in," Josh answered.

"Everything set up. I'm texting the address. Ms. Elodie will be waiting. Get Effie there, then hit me up. We need to get Ms. Elodie her money and the amount she want might take fucking days. You make the transaction and we'll reimburse you, Josh. Ophelia, call me when you, Josh, and Effie on the way."

"I'm going with Effie," I said, the minute the call disconnected.

"No, you're staying your fucking ass right here," Cash said. "We have some assholes to take care of."

"What the fuck does that mean?" For the first time since we arrived, I tuned in enough to hear Striker. Or, maybe, he hadn't spoken until now. "What assholes and where the fuck are we seeing to them?"

Daria touched me. "May I...is it okay if I go with them?"

"Your entire family can go," I said gently.

The last of my anger and dislike toward her died. I intended to push them to reveal the truth of Effie's father. For health reasons if nothing else. Besides, genealogy kits flooded the market. If Effie recovered, what if she decided to discover if she was one of the motherfuckers who carried Neanderthal DNA? What then? She had the chance to find out how her parents had lied to her in a variety of ways.

Stumbling upon the truth would be worse than her parents sitting her down and confessing.

Josh went to lift Effie into his arms, but I inserted myself in between him and the bar, and swept her up myself.

Unperturbed, Josh turned and headed out the door. I followed without question. Outside, many of the Dwellers remained. They were smoking and milling about. More than a few surrounded the van. However, they fell silent when they spotted me carrying Effie. The sudden gravity on their faces and the nods of acknowledgement surprised me, but I didn't feel so alone since I hadn't seen Dad and Drifter once we left the warehouse.

At the end of the block, Josh stopped at a black Escalade ESV. Ophelia scrambled into the cargo space. Josh nodded to me. Sighing, I laid Effie down and rested her head on Ophelia's lap.

"Need an escort, McCall?" a Death Dweller called. "Or you got this?"

"I can handle it," Josh answered, smiling at Cassie, then holding the door open as she climbed into the front passenger seat. "Thanks, though."

It took everything in me to stay calm and help Daria into the SUV, watch Lennon get in behind her, accept his son's pat on the back before he followed his parents inside, and step back.

"Go inside and have a drink," Josh said through the open window once he settled into the driver's seat. "Just trust us. We won't allow anything to happen to her. Right now, you have club business. Follow Cash's orders. He's a fucking jerk, but he's smart and he's good at what he does."

"Come on, Slice." Stretch's voice surprised me. "The sooner we settle everything, the sooner you can get to Effie."

He was right. Taking balls in hand, I flattened my palm against the SUV and knocked on it, then stepped out of the way. Josh reversed the short distance to the intersection, halted, then swerved forward and sped off.

Back inside, Striker greeted me with a punch. "Motherfucker, I told you I didn't want no fucking heat. Not only do the Sinners know you're hiding here, but I'm pretty fucking sure the cops are going to start breathing down our necks."

Most members of Red Rum's Austin chapter glared at me. Cash, Stretch, and the Death Dwellers glared at Striker.

"You got something to fucking say?" he snarled, glowering from Cash to Stretch.

"Yeah, fuckhead, I have a lot to say," Cash said, "but, lucky you, I don't have time."

"I could fucking shoot you," Striker roared. "I'm the president."

"Maybe, but you're not *our* president," Cash retorted. "Thank Christ. I would've left this motherfucker so far behind given your lack of loyalty and brotherhood."

"Enough, Cash," I inserted. He couldn't insult my fucking club. "You can't disrespect my club. This is how we operate. We pay our dues to National, but each chapter earns their own money, unless Riker gives an order like he did to me. We don't bring our problems to other chapters."

"The motherfucking national president brought the goddamn problem to *you*," Cash sneered. "Therefore, it should be an organizational problem. What the fuck is wrong with you assholes?"

"I take it you don't have any place to see to your enemies?" Stretch asked with a smidgeon of hope. "A basement? An attic? A dungeon?"

"My chapter has a small room and our mother chapter has an underground room," I said.

"Are we fucking at *your* chapter or the mother chapter, Slice?" Cash demanded.

"We don't make those fucking types of enemies here," Striker yelled. "We try not to off motherfuckers too often because we're such a small chapter, but when we do, we don't bring 'em on our fucking turf." He pointed a finger at me. "This stupid motherfucker botched the fucking interception. *He* made the enemy. Only reason Riker tried to smooth things over was because of Drifter." He glanced around. "Where is that motherfucker anyway?"

"At the warehouse with Goose and a few Dwellers," Cash said. "Cleaning shit up. Thank fuck it's a Sunday."

"This is my club," Striker roared. "Your interference is done. My law goes. I'm the leader."

"Then lead," Cash said. "Tell me what to do with the bodies. Tell me what to do with those bozos that need icing. If you wanted this goddamn problem to be local, advise your brother to have the local presidents give his fucking orders to their members. *Then* it's local."

Striker knocked me on the side of the head, and I growled. "You shouldn't have brought your fucking ass to that signing."

"You don't think I regret that decision?" I barked. "Effie...Effie's..." I couldn't fucking finish. I'd never been in a position where I had to choose between my club life and attending to a gravely injured person I loved. I felt torn in two, my head split between duty to my patch and the need to be at Effie's side.

"The bounty was on your fucking head," Striker continued. The derision on his face crucified me. "Pretty Boy Floyd. Nothing but a fuck-up. Don't belong in that fucking cut."

If Cash hadn't shoved me behind him, I would've struck Striker, and then that would've been my ass. He was an officer, while my classification was a special enforcer, above a regular member, but not on par with him.

"Let's just get those motherfuckers in here, deal with them, and hit the road before this ends badly," Saw said.

"That okay with you, Striker?" Cash gritted.

I could almost hear his teeth gnashing.

"Do it and then get the fuck out and don't set foot here again."

Ziggy and two unfamiliar Dwellers quickly marched in three bound and gagged motherfuckers. Their fear pleased me, though their attempts to speak worked on my fucking nerves.

"Shut them the fuck up," Striker ordered. Three of my brothers hurried over and knocked the fuckheads out with the butts of their guns.

Dislike blazing in his eyes, Cash looked at Striker. "You're offing them, *Prez*?"

Striker smirked at me. "We rescued his bitch. Let Pretty Boy Floyd do the honors."

I regretted leaving my machete in my saddlebag. After lopping off Dutch's head, I'd wiped the blade on my black jeans and hurried to Effie. Before I rode out, I shoved the knife away and left it there when we arrived here.

"I think all those camera flashes gave him amnesia." Striker laughed at his own joke. "He don't even know what the fuck to do anymore."

Suddenly, I understood Drifter's determination to join Riker in Vegas and Dad's insistence that he lead his own chapter. My twin belonged to the most powerful chapter and Dad fostered loyalty and unity. Perhaps, Striker agreed to start the Austin chapter because of the same competition that led him to his road name.

Once I'd been Floyd Elmont, then Pretty Boy Floyd, but I was Slice. I was a *biker* and I'd die for my colors. A part of me wished I had the chance to form my own chapter. If I brought in money, Riker would stay out of my way. My first order of business would be an alliance with the Death Dwellers.

I was *Slice*, the man Effie loved, even in a delirious state. Hopefully, I got the chance to prove myself worthy.

I studied the three unconscious men, wishing they were aware they didn't have long to live.

Cash followed my line of vision, sipped from a bottle of beer, then took a drag of his cigarette. "You don't need a knife to slice a motherfucker. Broken glass works, too. Jagged metal. Even hard plastic."

He was right.

"Head shots are quick and easy, but not nearly as satisfying," he continued, smoked again, then finished his beer and held out the bottle to me.

Smiling, I took it and got to work.

Effie

Once I awakened in my hospital room and Mom, Dad, Cass, and Heath filled in my blank spots, it all rushed back to me, including Dutch and Buck's gory deaths. I had a host of sprains, bruises, breaks, and contusions.

I couldn't believe how my sister hugged me so tightly and burst into tears. Hopefully, it was a new beginning for us. Dad and Heath hovered. And my mom?

For the rest of my life, I'd carry her words with me.

"Effie, my darling, I'd never been so terrified in the hours you were gone."

Hours? It had felt like days.

"I've made so many mistakes with you along the way. From this moment forward, I won't interfere with your life. As long as you're safe and happy. If you want Slice, I support your decision one hundred percent. I love you. I should never have raised my hand to you. That was unworthy of me. I lived my life. You deserve no less. I hope you can forgive me one day."

"You're forgiven, Mom," I said hoarsely. "I love you so much."

Over the course of the next few hours, I noted the luxury of my surroundings. Shades of creams and browns decorated the expansive room. My bed stood against a wall midway between the left side with a dining table and four chairs and the right side that had a sofa, loveseat, and coffee table. A huge TV hung on the wall across from me.

If not for all the medical equipment, I would've sworn we weren't in a hospital.

A hospital. Damn it! The police must've been called.

"It's taken care of, love," Mom reassured me when I asked her. "Everyone's safe."

Trusting her, I fell back to sleep.

When I awakened, I asked for Slice and continued to do so intermittently throughout the next hours. I wanted to see Slice. Or even receive a call from him. But nothing.

My family had just finished dinner. A divine meal that included beef, roasted potatoes, salad, and cobbler. None of which I tasted, since my doctor allowed me to have soft foods only earlier today. An improvement from the liquid diet. I wasn't sure if it was my abused throat, my broken ribs, or my dehydration that called for those dietary choices, but it was horrific.

After pushing aside my tray, I left Slice another message. Yeah, my pride was out the window, but I wanted to see for myself that he was fine. Even if he never wanted to see me again afterward.

My door opened and a dark-haired man peeped in.

"Josh!" Cassie called happily.

Smiling, *Josh* walked in. Oh my. He was almost as gorgeous as Slice. I was so busy staring at him, I didn't notice Cash until he stood at the foot of my bed.

"He's another asshole you don't want to admire," he grumbled. "That shit goes to his fucking head, too."

"Don't hate me 'cause I'm beautiful," Josh quipped. "You took all Dad's looks. My mother saved me."

Cash flipped him off. Despite my despondency, I laughed. Citing addiction concerns, the doctor was also cutting back on my pain meds after a mere three days.

Thankfully, I had a high pain tolerance.

"That's a beautiful sound, darlin'," Josh drawled. "I'm so glad to hear it, considering the state you were in when I drove you here."

My humor fled.

"He has a big mouth, doesn't he, Effie?" a new, vaguely familiar voice said.

Mom and Cassie squealed.

Cash stepped aside and my chin almost dropped to my chest. There, before me, stood Sloane Mason, a freaking guitar strapped to him.

"The McCall Monsters—" His finger wagged between Josh and Cash— "are horrendous assholes."

"Hey, fuckhead, my little sister is a McCall," Cash barked.

"The sweet one," he said, and focused on me. "Ophelia begged me to visit you, Effie. Can I call you Effie?"

I nodded, speechless.

"Any woman who puts up with that motherfucker—" he nodded to Cash— "deserves her every wish granted. She's a fucking saint."

Mom, Cassie, and I exchanged glances and giggled.

"Had I wanted to decline Fee, Slice made a very compelling argument."

"Sl-slice?" I whispered.

Sloane nodded. He straightened his guitar and adjusted the frets, holding up a pick that I hadn't realized was in his hand. Two more men walked through my opened door.

Joy seeped into me. Slice had finally arrived, but then he smiled. It was different, more cynical. When Slice grinned, his entire face lit up. His twin's was more guarded.

"I'm Drifter," he introduced, then nodded to the older man. "Dad. Goose," he added.

I knew of them, but I'd never met either before.

Drifter looked at Sloane and nodded.

"The fire inside me," he began to croon to a soft melodic rhythm. "The love that I feel."

Slice walked in. The moment our gazes met, all my fear and worry evaporated. In his eyes, I saw what *I* felt. Respect and admiration. And love. I recognized it because I finally accepted I *did* want what my parents shared.

Slice reached my bedside, bent, and kissed me. "Hey, sweetheart."

"Hey," I said softly.

He brushed his fingers through my hair and I leaned into his touch.

"I thought you were done with me," I said.

"Never. You're stuck with me, Effie." He straightened and dug in his pocket, pulling out a ring. I gasped. Sloane continued singing *Inferno*.

"It's not an engagement ring—yet," Slice said fiercely. "It's a promise to love and cherish you. When the time's right, then I'll propose." He kissed me. "I love you, Effie."

"I love you, too, Slice," I whispered.

"So what do you say?"

Giggling, I held out my hand. "Yes! Yes! Yes!"

We kissed to a round of applause. I'd never been happier. Looking into Slice's eyes, I knew he felt the same.

Effie

The road to recovery wasn't an easy one and included surgery to repair the damage to my broken nose. Long after the physical wounds healed, the mental scars remained. The terror of my kidnapping. The bone-chilling dread as I questioned if I'd survive. The disgust whenever it dawned on me I'd taken a man's life. In the heat of the moment, it hadn't mattered. It was me or him. I understood that I'd had no choice. Sometimes, though, it was all too much. So much gore. The blood. The head.

It all stuck with me. Each time I remembered, I shook and shivered.

However, despite my trauma and though it was hard, an invaluable support system surrounded me. My mother stuck to her word, prioritizing my happiness and safety over hers. My father followed suit, and even Cassie stepped up and made herself available if I needed to talk. She was still with that nitwit, but hey, progress was progress. Heath took a leave of absence from his job and had just returned to New York a few days ago after four months in Corpus Christi.

With all my family's much appreciated support, Slice helped me the most. He asked for time off and Goose agreed. Saw and Ziggy got permission from their chapter president for Slice to stay at the club, since Mom and Dad wouldn't hear of him staying under our roof. They also cited Heath's presence. *Perhaps,* they claimed, if Heath hadn't been there, they *might've* allowed Slice to use that room.

Bullshit, but I allowed them to believe their own lies.

Slice attended to my every need. He and Heath bonded. Josh McCall made a few calls and arranged an interview for Heath with a Fortune 500 company that he'd been dying to work for. It was why he left before the end of the summer.

Ophelia called regularly and checked to see if we needed anything. Although Slice couldn't spend the night, he, Saw, and Ziggy became fixtures at our dinner table. They regaled Mom with stories that would feed her imagination for years to come.

In my darkest hour, though, Slice was there to comfort me for the first few weeks. He'd been immersed in violence for years and shared his own experiences and coping mechanisms. He told me about the first time he saw a life taken, and the first time he took a life, and described in detail how he felt about both. It was a fucked up way for us to deepen our bond, but ultimately, his understanding brought us closer together.

So close, in fact, that I transferred to a school in Oklahoma.

Breaking the news to my parents wasn't easy. By their expressions, I knew they held back a wealth of words. Heath backed up my decision and helped me choose the right university and fill out my paperwork. He sat with me during the meeting with Mom and Dad. His presence might've helped to keep them from losing it. Although Slice had already returned to Oklahoma City, he supported my decision. My parents knew they were outnumbered with my brother and Slice on my side.

Finally, Mom asked me to consider three things: self-defense classes, always carrying a stun gun and pepper spray, and counseling before and after my move.

I was on board with the first two, but hesitant about therapy. I didn't want to share what occurred and incriminate Slice, Drifter, Goose, Saw, Ziggy, and their respective club members. They'd saved me, and I wouldn't repay them by telling a stranger of their justified crime.

Of course, my father agreed with Mom, so I didn't reveal my decision to protect Slice. Heath knew, though, and he squeezed my hand in reassurance when Mom lifted her brow and awaited my agreement. Instead, I just smiled and nodded, promising to consider her advice. Now, she believed I couldn't find a therapist who was the right fit for me and encouraged me to look in Oklahoma City since Corpus Christi apparently had such slim pickings.

Despite her progress, Mom would forever be Mom, offering suggestions and a tad bit clueless.

I loved her with all my heart, though. That was why the first thing I did when I touched down in the Sooner State was send her a selfie and a text declaring my arrival.

Once I rented a cart and collected my belongings from baggage claim, I trudged to passenger pickup to wait for Slice, so we could head over to our new apartment. He'd FaceTime me while he toured several apartments before we chose one together and he placed the deposit. I'd never visited his city and he wanted me to like where we'd live together.

I paced around as I searched for his recently purchased black Ford-150. He said it was for me to drive on the days he couldn't usher me around on the back of his bike.

Now that I was there, time crept by. Where was he already?

I was too excited to stay in one place. I'd dreamed of a future with Slice for so long. I'd longed to live my life as I saw fit—Mom had lived *her* life. I'd never understood her obsessive protectiveness toward me, but everything fell into place when it was meant to.

Finally, Slice's truck gunned into view. Clapping, I bounced up and down at the music blaring from the sunroof. I focused on the driver.

Slice. AKA my boyfriend.

A goofy grin spread across my face. Slice was my boyfriend. Butterflies swooped in my belly at the thought.

He pulled up beside me. I'd intentionally dressed colorful, so he could easily spot me. Throwing the truck in park, he hopped out and strolled to me. His long, beautiful hair had no tether, flowing freely around him. Underneath his denim cut, a short-sleeved T-shirt stretched across his muscles. Powerful thighs outlined his jeans, and my nipples hardened at the bulge in his crotch.

Wrapping his strong arms around my waist, he kissed the top of my head and held me close. Burying my nose in the crook of his neck, I inhaled his scent and hugged him, reveling in his nearness.

"I missed you, sweetheart," he breathed into my hair.

"Ditto." As I sank into his embrace, it was the only word I could manage.

During my flight, doubts assailed me. Not only was I moving away from home and leaving my family, I was moving to another state, a place I'd never visited. I wondered if I made the right choice or if I was an impulsive idealist. Yet how secure and cherished I felt in his arms arrested my fears.

I definitely made the right choice.

He pulled away ever so slightly, bent down and kissed me. It was brief and chaste, leaving me wanting more, and desperately wishing we were at the apartment.

"C'mon, Effie," he said, releasing me. He transferred my bags from the cart to the truck bed. "Let's go home. I can't wait to show you our place."

Home.

The word resonated, filling me with giddiness so intense, I giggled. My home was with Slice now, and I wouldn't have it any other way.

Idle chatter and off-key singing highlighted the drive to the apartment. We took turns picking songs to play on the aux cord. Neither of us could carry a tune, but we still had fun.

My new home was an hour away from the airport, nestled in a quiet neighborhood brimming with manicured mid-century architecture. According to GPS, we were twenty minutes away from downtown, a slice of suburbia amid the city. Towering oaks lined the street, creating a canopy that filtered out the sunlight. The five-story complex was constructed of red bricks with white siding. Small balconies graced each unit. Residents of all ages milled about, walking their dogs, jogging around, and playing games.

Admittedly, it shocked me. Slice had only sent pictures of the interior and withheld the exact address, likely a safety measure in case our texts were compromised. I had expected us to be in the heart of Oklahoma City, not the picturesque outskirts.

"This neighborhood looks so nice," I stated as Slice parked the truck.

He cocked a brow. "Did you think I'd choose a shitty area?"

Fuck, was that the impression my words gave?

"No, no, of course not." My face heated at my blunder. While I saw the inside of the apartments before we chose, I'd never seen the surroundings. "I just didn't expect the area to look like an inspiration for Norman Rockwell."

"Didn't he mostly paint holiday and historical shit?"

"His paintings try to capture an idealistic version of the lives of everyday Americans. This," I stated, indicating the area with my hand, "is an ideal for many people."

He let out a low whistle as he cut off the engine, grinning at me. "My girl knows her shit, huh?"

My girl.

I'd never tire of hearing that.

"I was at the top of my class in honors art class, baby," I bragged.

He chuckled and I giggled.

Like a true gentleman, he opened my door for me, holding my hand as he helped me out of the truck. He grabbed my two oversized duffle bags but allowed me to roll my suitcase, so I didn't feel like a complete burden.

I took in the minute details as we walked to the building. Professional landscaping, community benches, and quiet corners all added to the cozy atmosphere. I couldn't wait to snap some pictures and send them to my parents, although I'd refrain from posting anything online that gave away my location.

I'd learned the dangers of that the hard way.

Once we reached the third floor, Slice set the bags down, reached into the pocket of his jeans and pulled out a set of keys.

"Your set is on your nightstand," he said, fumbling with the keys before he successfully unlocked the door. He allowed me to enter first. The space was open, and natural light streamed through the large windows. A comfy-looking sectional faced a wall-mounted TV, a small bookshelf below the device. The kitchen was small but filled with modern appliances and a tiny island. Near the hallway, a dining table with two chairs was tucked in a corner.

Everything was orderly, but lacked personal touches, something I'd remedy. Ideas populated my mind. Throw pillows and blankets on the couch, a plant on the dining table, pretty artwork on the walls, and a fluffy rug to take up some of the empty space on the floor. However, home décor was an agenda for another day.

"What do you think?" he asked as I walked to the sliding door and peeked outside.

He'd managed to fit two lawn chairs and a little table on the small balcony. Already, I knew I'd be spending a lot of time there.

"This is amazing, Slice." I faced him and smiled. We hadn't seen each other in almost six weeks. Before he left and once I recovered, we'd gone on dates, including detours to motels. Slice had also introduced me to sex on the back of his bike. I didn't want him to think his hard work was unappreciated, but I wanted to feel his strong arms around me. My anxiety flared and I returned to topic. "When can we go shopping for decorations?"

The corner of his lips tilted into a smile and he shook his head, nodding to the room at large. "Amazing, huh?"

Though his tone was teasing, I rolled my eyes. "Every home needs decoration, so hush."

"If you insist. C'mon, let me show you our room."

We abandoned my luggage by the door. He led me down the short hallway where three doorways stood. He pushed open the one straight ahead and revealed a tidy bedroom. The walls were a calming shade of pastel blue, while the comforter was a deeper navy. Like the rest of the apartment, it was admirably neat, but in dire need of personalization.

Slice watched me closely as I examined the room. "What do you think?" he asked.

"Didn't peg you as a neat freak."

He opened his arms and I happily stepped into his embrace.

Those strong arms wrapped around my waist, holding me close to his chest. "You thought I was a slob who lived in filth?"

"A busy guy who couldn't bother with housework," I corrected, licking my lips and holding his gaze.

His eyes followed my tongue and he groaned. He leaned in, capturing my lips. I melted into him, my hands fisting his shirt. As our tongues met, everything felt right with the world. This new chapter of my life seemed straight out of one of my mom's romance novels. After ups and downs, the hero gets the girl, and they find their happily-ever-after.

The kiss roughened and turned more demanding. I matched his urgency and tangled my fingers in his silky hair.

"Slice," I breathed against his lips.

He grabbed my ass and I gasped.

Capturing my wrist, he guided my hand to the bulge in his jeans. A wave of heat swept through me at the feel of his thick hardness.

"Feel what you do to me, baby? That's all for you."

Desire jolted through me. Suddenly, the urge to taste him overtook me. Blowjobs weren't my expertise, but you only perfected a skill with practice. His tongue had brought me intense pleasure, and I desperately wanted to return the favor. After a moment of hesitation, I dropped to my knees and grabbed his belt buckle, but didn't undo it as smoothly as I imagined.

"Shit," I mumbled as I struggled.

My cheeks heated at his deep chuckle.

"Don't worry about it, sweetheart—"

"Shut up," I ordered, glaring up at him. "I want to."

His eyes darkened and he licked his lips. "Who am I to stop you? I've dreamed of my dick in your mouth."

He removed the troublesome belt and tossed it aside. My fingers deftly unzipped his jeans, freeing his erection. Not wasting a second, I wrapped my lips around his cock tip and swirled my tongue.

"Fuck," he groaned.

Encouraged, I savored his salty flavor and took him deeper, stretching my lips around his girth. I noted what elicited the most reactions, repeating every action that made him swear under his breath. His muscles tightened and I understood his orgasm neared. I desperately wanted him to let go, so I took him deeper until his trimmed pubic hair tickled my nose. Each of my gags reminded me to relax my throat and breathe through my nose. Slice's enormous cock made him almost impossible to deepthroat. However, I managed, and I loved the way he filled my mouth so completely.

"Fuck, Effie...feels so fucking good," he panted. He held my head and pumped in and out of my mouth.

His breathing harshened and his muscles tautened. I sucked him harder. A guttural groan left him and his cock pulsed as his cum flooded my mouth. I swallowed every drop, breathing in his scent, my head spinning at his heady taste.

Pulling back, I looked at him through the sweep of my lashes, admiring his parted lips and hooded eyes. He helped me to my feet, and to my surprise, kissed me. In my limited experience, guys weren't fond of kissing after blowjobs. Then again, they also hadn't enjoyed going down on me, whereas Slice was a certified munch. Clearly, he was a different caliber of man.

His tongue pushed into my mouth. I'm sure he tasted himself on my tongue. His hands were everywhere, roaming over my curves before homing in on my breasts. As he groped my tits, he walked me to the bed. When my thighs hit the mattress, we separated, hurriedly undressing. Once we were both nude, he pushed me onto the bed, his eyes burning with hunger.

"Missed you so fucking much," he growled, before his mouth descended on my nipple.

I moaned, arching into him as his tongue swirled around the pebbling bud. His hand slipped between my legs, two fingers easing inside of me as he worshipped my tits, lavishing each breast with plenty of attention. My hips bucked when his thumb met my clit, my cunt clinching around his invading digits.

"Don't stop, please," I whimpered, my orgasm rapidly building.

Try as I might, I couldn't replicate the pleasure Slice gave me with my own fingers, and I was too nervous to own a sex toy in my parents' house. It left me sensitive and wanting, gasping and writhing each time he moved his fingers.

He twisted his fingers just right, stimulating my G-spot and curling my toes. All the while, his thumb rubbed circles over my clit, and his mouth worshipped my breasts. The combined sensation hurled me toward ecstasy. He added a third finger.

"Slice," I screamed. "Oh, holy fuck!" My body jerking, I gushed around him, stars dancing in my vision.

Slice released my nipple with a wet 'pop,' his eyes glued to my face as I rode out my orgasm. He gentled his motions, his hand finally stilling when the pleasure bordered on overstimulation.

"I need to be inside you," he breathed, positioning myself between my thighs.

"I want you inside me," I replied, licking my lips as he stroked his hard cock, spreading his precum around his shaft.

He must've gathered watching him touch himself was arousing. He began putting on more of a show for me. An idea spawned in my head, and before he could insert himself, I took advantage of his idling and pushed him down.

His hands flew to my hips as I straddled him. "What are you doing, sweetheart?"

"Riding you," I said simply and sank down on him.

We both moaned. The way his cock stretched me made my head loll. Being on top not only allowed me to set the pace but helped him to go deeper and hit every pressure point.

"Fuck, you're so tight," he groaned, his eyes mere slits.

I started moving my hips, resting my hands on his chest to steady myself. It took me a moment to find a rhythm that felt good for us both, but when I did, bliss exploded through my body. Not wanting to offend my neighbors on day one, I buried my face in his neck to muffle my moans.

"Oh my gosh!" I whimpered.

"That's it, baby," he growled, his grip on my hips digging into my skin as he guided my movements. "Keep fucking me like that."

He grew more demanding, so I moved my hips faster, my body coiling tighter as I rode him like there was no tomorrow. His cock twitched inside me. Meeting me stroke for stroke, he thrust into me. The primal echo of skin slapping against skin bounced off the bedroom walls. Fucking quietly was an impossible task. It simply wasn't feasible, with such electricity racing through my body.

"I'm close," I announced, resting my forehead against his and looking into his eyes.

"Come for me, Effie," he demanded, inserting a hand between our sweaty bodies and teasing my clit. "Soak my fucking cock, sweetheart."

His ragged voice, naughty demand, and delicious touch catapulted me over the edge. My orgasm ripped through me and I cried out. My body convulsed, and my nails dug into his shoulders, leaving crescent-shaped indents.

"Fuck, yes!" he roared, his hips slamming into mine one final time before his cum flooded my walls.

Thank God for birth control, the proud sponsor of worry-free creampies.

When my pleasure started to wane, I collapsed onto his chest. Trembling, I struggled to catch my breath. Slice slung an arm around my waist, holding me close while we recovered from our earth-shattering orgasms.

"That was..." I started, my voice shaking.

My words trailed into a breathy laugh, my head still spinning. That was worth the wait, and the best housewarming present I could ask for. We had no limit on how often we made love now that we lived together. The realization thrilled me to no end.

"Incredible," he finished, kissing the top of my head before tilting my chin up to look me in the eyes. "You're incredible, Effie. I'm so fucking happy you're finally here with me."

My heart fluttered at his words. I smiled up at him, my body still tingling from the aftershocks of my climax.

"I'm happy I'm here, too." I lifted myself and brushed my lips over his. "I missed you so much."

Video calls and text messages hadn't been enough to satisfy my need for him in the last few weeks. Nothing compared to his presence, his scent, and his skin against mine.

We'd already been through the fire. Undoubtedly, we'd face more ups and downs in our relationship; it was only natural. But I didn't care. I loved him and he loved me. Come what may, I was eager to spend the rest of my life by his side.

Effie

Eight months later...

As a child, nothing made me feel more special than breakfast in bed. Every year on my birthday, my mother prepared blueberry pancakes and stuck a single candle in the middle no matter the age I turned. She also served me sliced fruit, bacon, and orange juice, delivered to me on a tray. While I enjoyed my meal, my family assembled around me with their gifts. We repeated the same routine with Cassie, Heath,

Mom, and Dad, creating an expectation of breakfast in bed during special occasions.

For my birthday and our anniversary, Slice continued the tradition, so I returned the favor on his birthday. However, living with Slice revealed something even better than breakfast delivered to you in bed: head.

Slice's mouth was a godsend, and an orgasm a day kept the bitch in me at bay. So, starting the day off with a hot tongue gliding through my folds almost guaranteed the day would be a good one.

Today, I'd graduate. A good tongue-lashing on my clit would get me nice and chipper.

As pleasure replaced my sleepiness, I threaded my fingers through his long hair. He sucked my clit into his mouth and I gasped.

"Fuck," I breathed, moving my hips to the rhythm of his tongue.

"That's it, use me, baby," he murmured against my mound, making no effort to stop my erratic grinding.

Humping his face was bad enough. Then he slipped two fingers inside my heat, curling them as he made out with my bundle of nerves, and I whined like a bitch in heat. Guiding a leg over his shoulder, he stroked my G-spot while mouthing my pussy, determined to throw me over the edge. He smiled against me as my legs trembled and tension built in my core.

"I'm close!" I cried, my head thrown back in ecstasy.

He lightly nibbled on my clit, the slight sting sending me hurling over the edge. My mind went blank, my feminine sap exploding from me and soaking Slice's face. He groaned in approval, removing his fingers and tonguing my pussy hole, collecting every drop. My body shook violently. As much as I enjoyed his tongue, I had no choice but to shove his forehead away when his attention grew too much to handle.

He drew away with a frustrated moan, a trail of slick extending between my pussy and Slice's mouth. A shriek of humiliation left me at the sight, my body flushing. I wasn't a prude, but nor was I as freaky as Slice, so the sight made me clamp my hands over my face.

He chuckled, grabbing my wrists and dragging my hands away. "Good morning, sweetheart," he murmured, kissing each palm before releasing me. "Big day today."

Fuck.

I started twisting my hands. Big days always made me nervous, and after years of studying and a lifetime of dreaming, I'd finally have my degree.

"Yeah," I said simply, looking to the bedroom door as a delicious aroma wafted to me. "What are you cooking?"

A simple redirection to distract myself for the moment.

"Ham and cheese quiche," he answered, rolling off the bed and stretching. "Should be ready in the next fifteen minutes."

My stomach grumbled, and my mouth watered. The promise of food propelled me to my feet.

"A biker, a model, a cook. A proper renaissance man," I teased.

He swept me into his arms and I giggled.

"All for you, baby," he said, brushing his lips over mine. "I'll go get coffee on."

"Or," I began, clinging to him when he tried to pull away. "We can take a quick shower, and I can return your morning surprise."

Slice grinned, his eyes sparkling. "What the graduate wants, the graduate gets."

With zero effort, he scooped me into his arms and headed toward the bathroom, his touch easing my nerves.

A lot of changes took place after I moved to OKC. Learning the identity of my biological father was the biggest. If Slice hadn't insisted, I might never have found out about Ezekial Lawson, my dead biker father with the same last name as a hero in one of Mom's books.

At first, the revelation crushed me, but with Slice's help I realized Lennon Monroe might not have made me, but he was my daddy. My father.

Dad.

I'd never know the relationship I might've had with Ezekial, but Dad stepped up to the plate, took care of me, and loved me as much as he loved Heath and Cassie. Neither Mom nor Dad explained what led to her affair. He'd forgiven her and he hadn't held it against her or me.

Together, Mom, Dad, Slice, and I made a pact to keep the secret between us. It wouldn't matter to Heath, but Cassie was a different story.

Slice retired from modeling, although Mom continued churning out bestsellers and attending book signings.

I wasn't sure why this ran through my head as I sat amongst my fellow graduates. Perhaps, it served as a distraction.

The black gown concealing my blue dress felt as heavy as the cap atop my head. In the best way possible, anxiety riddled me as I waited to hear my name. When I finally transferred to Oklahoma State University a few days after the Fall semester began, I worried that my graduation would be delayed even more. I'd had to withdraw during my recovery. Fortunately, all my credits transferred effortlessly. Besides playing catch-up with assignments during the first three weeks, everything was smooth sailing.

Though I graduated on time, my school load had been intense.

The weather played nice today and reflected the cheery moves of the attendees. The sun shone brightly, and a pleasant breeze blew outside. Inside the stadium, however, the many bodies and my nerves made the environment suffocating. Time seemed to drag as I waited for my name to be called. Besides a study buddy here and a lab partner there, I wasn't familiar with many of my classmates. Still, I clapped for everyone, adding an extra 'oomph' for those I did know.

Finally, the moment I was waiting for arrived.

"Effie Monroe," the announcer called.

As I walked to the stage, my heart beat a rapid tattoo at the applause.

"That's my daughter!" my mother yelled, and I smiled.

Dad, Heath, Cassie, and Slice accompanied her, though they were more reserved in their cheering, making it harder to make out their voices.

I shook the hands of everyone on stage, accepted my degree, and posed for a picture. The moment I had been waiting for was over within a minute, but the brief time didn't lessen the sense of accomplishment I felt. I was a second-generation college graduate, and I could not be prouder of myself.

With my degree in hand, the rest of the ceremony passed quickly. The speeches, songs, and the endless procession of my classmates blurred together as I thought about the next chapter in my life.

Riker finally okayed Slice's new road name and promoted him to top enforcer. I clapped and cheered at the ceremony when they retired his 'Pretty Boy' patch and he officially became 'Slice'. Drifter, Raider, Dolph, Desmond, Saw, Ziggy, Cash, and Stretch even made the trip to OKC. I'd never partied so much in my life. Later, I learned Red Rum and Satan's Sinners reached an uneasy peace agreement, which had been negotiated by Slice.

Although I missed my family, and Corpus Christi, I was so happy for Slice and proud to be his.

Before I knew it, the graduation ceremony ended and locating my family took me a moment. I nearly screamed when a hand clamped down on my shoulder, my heart rate spiking. The relief I felt when I saw it was Slice was immeasurable.

"You scared me," I complained, returning his kiss.

He was quite affectionate and loved PDA as much as me.

"Sorry, babe," he murmured against my lips.

"Eww," Cassie said, making me pull away from my boyfriend to stick my tongue out at her.

"Be quiet," I ordered, nestling into Slice as he wrapped an arm around my shoulder. "You and Chad are always making out in front of us."

She huffed, crossing her arms over her chest. "Don't even say his stupid name. I'm so done with that jerk."

Mmhmm. I'd heard that a million times. As much as I prayed she meant it, I doubt her current sentiment would stick.

"Girls, enough squabbling," my father said when he, Heath, and my mom came into view.

"There's my little scholar," Mom squealed, barreling into me with surprising force. "Oh, I'm so proud of you, honey!"

Despite her attempting to squeeze the life out of me, I returned her hug and grinned. "Thank you, Mom."

We stayed like that for a few seconds before she moved away. She looked at Slice, Heath, and then my father. A frown tugged at her lips. "None of you have given Effie her flowers yet."

Startled, I peered from one to the other.

Dad carried different colored daisies, Heath had tulips, and Slice held a bouquet of my favorite flower—red carnations. It was a mystery to me how I missed all the beautiful flowers. Out of respect, I took my father's first.

"Thank you, Dad," I said as I tucked the bouquet under my arms, giving him a hug that was briefer than the one I shared with my mother.

He sniffled, the sound surprising me. "You're all grown up."

"She's been grown for, like, four years now," Cassie grumbled.

We ignored her. I pulled away and Mom took my place, whispering to my father as I took my brother's flowers, smiling at his tight hug. I turned to Slice and grabbed the flowers he offered.

"They're gorgeous," I murmured, kissing his cheek.

The heels I wore might've been a bitch on my feet, but they gave me a nice height boost.

"Took you long enough to notice them," he replied.

"Okay, enough lovey-dovey shit, I'm hungry!" Cassie declared. I rolled my eyes. "Let's get to the restaurant before I starve to death."

"Sweetie, this is Effie's day," Mom said, far gentler than I wanted to be.

"And it'll be Effie's day when we get to the restaurant," she countered.

"She's right. We can take pictures and all of that there," I conceded, not wanting my graduation to turn into a shitshow.

Cassie really tried to act better, but that only lasted until I moved away. She would forever want to be the center of attention, even on a day when I was supposed to be celebrated. But hey, at least she came when her presence hadn't been guaranteed because of Chad. Look on the bright side and all that jazz.

Dinner was a nice affair. We discussed little of essence, but nothing sparked arguments, so I took that as a win. Slice rented one of the restaurant's private rooms, insisted we splurge on whatever we wanted, and paid for the entire thing. Once we shoved the food down our hatch, I received my presents.

Cassie thoroughly redeemed herself when she presented me with a one-hundred-dollar gift card. It wouldn't buy much, but it was more than she'd spent on a present for me in a long, long time.

I aimed a small smile her way before tucking the card away in my clutch. "This is nice, Cass, thank you."

She nodded in response. I peeked at Slice, who was quietly watching the exchange. He winked at me when our eyes met, and I blew a kiss in response.

"Again, with the PDA," Cassie complained.

We all ignored her.

Mom was nearly bouncing off her seat as my father handed me a gift bag. The colorful envelope resting on top of the wrapped gifts caught my attention, so I opened that first. It was a generic graduation card with my parents' signatures, but the five hundred dollars inside more than made up for the lack of personalization.

"The money is from me," Dad announced proudly.

Mom huffed. "I told him he should've gotten you something more personal, but—"

"It's fine, this is perfect," I said, unable to stop grinning. "Thank you so much, Dad."

"You're welcome, sweetie," Dad said with smug satisfaction. Mom rolled her eyes, but he ignored her and said, "I knew you'd love it."

Duh. Who didn't like money? Cold, hard, cash might not have a lot of thought behind it, but it was always appreciated.

"Open mine now," Mom ordered.

My immediate compliance restored her cheeriness.

The gift bag contained three beautifully wrapped presents. The first was a small photo album, containing pictures of me during the first day of every educational year from kindergarten to twelfth grade. It had been a tradition for Mom to drag Heath, Cassie, and me out of bed extra early, and snap photos of us before we went off to school to celebrate us starting another grade. To my surprise, flipping through the photos made me a bit teary-eyed. I blinked rapidly, not wanting to cry and ruin my makeup.

"This is so sweet, Mom," I said with a sniffle.

"Aw, sweetie, don't cry yet; you'll make me cry!" she exclaimed, passing me a napkin.

"Let me see little you, baby," Slice requested as I dabbed at my eyes.

That dried my tears quickly. I cringed at the thought of my boyfriend seeing my pimply middle school self or my high school emo phase.

"I'd rather—"

Cassie snatched the album from my hand and handed it to him. "Here you go, Slice."

To his credit, he didn't immediately open it, instead fixing her with a glare before refocusing on me, picking up on my demeanor. "I don't have to look at them now, sweetheart."

"No, it's okay." I threw Cassie a dirty look as he opened the book.

She just shrugged.

While Slice looked at my childhood pictures, I moved on to the next gift. Unwrapping the next present and revealing the state-of-the-art camera made me squeal. It put my basic digital camera to shame and included its own built-in Wi-Fi, 9-point autofocus system, and high-resolution megapixel CMOS sensor. Put simply, it was amazing. Within seconds, I set the camera down, jumped to my feet, and hugged my mom.

"Thank you, oh my gosh!"

She laughed and returned the hug, reaching over and pulling the bag closer. "You're welcome, darling. One thing left."

That last thing turned out to be a stunning jewelry set, consisting of a silver vine necklace with diamond flowers, and matching earrings.

"It's gorgeous," I breathed, lifting the jewelry closer to the light to admire them. "How much was this?"

"You know she won't tell you, Effie," Cassie said with a petulant pout. "Besides, you got more than me when I graduated high school, so why does it matter?"

"Only a car, poor you," I replied, my voice dripping with sarcasm as my temper started to rise.

"It was used."

Heath shook his head. "Classic Cass," he said, resembling Dad more by the day. "Never grateful for shit."

Cassie tossed her red hair and sniffed. "You don't understand, Heath. You got a new car—"

"That I fucking worked for," Heath snapped. I maintained she and Mom drove Heath to move as far away as possible. "Mom and Dad matched what I saved. I had to take care of my monthly payment. You had zero expense. Not even insurance. They paid that, too."

"On a *used* car," Cassie reiterated.

I growled. "It was more than you had before, and in good condition, so stop bitchin'. Mom and Dad also paid for a year's rent when you graduated community college, so—"

"Children, please!" Dad said, fixing us with a hard stare. "Cassie, stop ruining your sister's day." He pointed from Heath to me. "You two, stop adding fuel to the fire."

That caught Slice's attention, his gaze snapping from the photo album to my father. "Effie isn't doing shit—"

The look I gave him silenced him, though he didn't return to flipping through the pictures.

"Enough squabbling," Mom ordered, before redirecting the conversation back to my jewelry. "I thought of you the moment I saw it, Effie. You can make them heirlooms and give them to your daughter when she graduates or wear them when you get married. You've always wanted a botanical garden wedding, so they'll be perfect."

I looked at Slice, trying to imagine what he'd look like in a tuxedo. Handsome, no doubt; I didn't think he was capable of making anything look bad. An image of him standing by a wedding arch as Dad escorted me down the aisle popped into my head. Slice would look dapper and stare at me with hearts in his eyes.

Warmth filling me, I sighed dreamily.

"My turn," Slice announced.

He reached into his jacket pocket and retrieved a ring box. My heart started to beat faster. He stood from his chair and walked to me, dropping down on one knee.

"Effie Alessia Monroe, will you do me the honor of becoming my wife?"

A flurry of emotions swarmed me. Shock, excitement, anxiety, and most of all, overwhelming love. My eyes misted once more. This time, I didn't try to dry the happy tears sliding down my cheeks. I nodded frantically, holding out my left hand, so he'd remove the promise ring and slide the engagement ring onto my finger.

"Yes, yes, a thousand times yes!" I cried.

Laughter burst from me at the weight of the ring on my finger.

It was unreal, everything I'd ever dreamed of. For a moment, I feared it was too joyous for reality and was tempted to pinch myself to see if I was dreaming.

A grin spread across Slice's handsome face and my heart fluttered. He rose up, sweeping me into his arms as my family clapped. Heath's applause was the most genuine. Cassie's was slow, almost sarcastic, my father's was polite, while my mother screamed and bounced with such elation, I reached for her.

We hugged tightly.

"I love you, Mom."

"I love you more, Effie Monroe, soon-to-be Elmont."

Mom released me and Slice set me on my feet, hugging me to him.

Everyone faded into the background as Slice embraced me. I clung to him, breathing in his addictive scent.

He kissed me tenderly. "I have one more present, sweetheart. I'll be right back."

"What is it?" Mom breathed once Slice walked out.

I couldn't imagine, but I had a couple ideas. "Maybe it's Sloane Mason again to serenade us as we take our first dance as an engaged couple? Or Ophelia flew in?"

It had bummed me out big time when none of our friends attended my graduation. Even if Ophelia couldn't make it, I'd expected Drifter, Goose, Ziggy, and Saw. Yeah, they were still Death Dwellers, but they'd become like family.

Slice returned carrying two red garment boxes wrapped with black ribbon. I felt like a bitch at my disappointment, so I plastered a smile on my face when he handed a box to me and a box to Mom.

Her eyes lit up. "For me?"

"As my soon to be mother-in-law," Slice said.

Mom squealed. "What is it?"

"You have to open it and find out, love," Dad called.

"Open yours, Effie," Mom encouraged, "so I can open mine."

"You first, Mom." I winced at my resigned tone. "Er, I've gotten so many presents already."

Slice's eyes twinkled.

Mom didn't hesitate to rip the box open. Her gasp reverberated through the private room.

"Oh my god!" she screamed.

"What—"

Before I asked the question, she held up a leather cut. Tears filled her eyes and her nose reddened. She flew to Slice and bear hugged him so tight, he groaned.

"Let us see it, Mom," Heath said, grinning.

Swiping at her cheeks, she turned the back toward us. *Mother-in-law of Slice* was written on it.

"I thought the cut would resemble yours, Slice," Dad said, revealing he'd known about Slice's present.

"Open yours, Effie," Slice said, ignoring my dad as Mom shrugged into her cut and squealed again.

Laughing, Dad took her into his arms and kissed her.

My heart pounding in anticipation, I copied Mom, tore away the ribbon on my box, and lifted the top. My cut was also leather with the words, *Property of Slice*.

"Bet that beats a fucking engagement ring, Effie," Saw said as he and Ziggy carried an ice chest in.

"Says you, fuckhead," Slice retorted as he helped me put my cut on.

I understood what Dad meant. Slice had a denim cut. It would've been nice to match.

"I won't ever spend that much money on no broad," Dolph complained, walking in with Drifter, Goose, Raider, and Desmond following.

"Who has the bud?" Raider asked.

"All right, fuckheads, behave," Goose ordered. He wagged a finger at the two Dweller boys. "Outlaw gave me permission to kick your ass if you fuck up Effie's celebration."

"Can you bring an ice chest in a fancy restaurant?" Cassie asked.

"No motherfucker'll stop us," Saw replied.

Ziggy pulled out a bag of weed, and I gasped.

Growling, Slice stormed over and snatched it from him, while Saw slapped the back of his head.

"What's going on in here?" Riker demanded, sauntering in and carrying a garment bag.

As uncomfortable as Striker made me, it couldn't compare to how I felt in Riker's presence. His soulless eyes chilled me.

Luckily, the guys congratulating me distracted me. Heath helped to pass out beers from Saw's ice chest. They toasted me and someone produced a Bluetooth speaker, hooked up their phone and provided loud music.

I expected management to throw us out, but that didn't happen.

We danced, talked, and drank. Even Cassie loosened up and Mom floated on a cloud, flitting from Dad, Riker, and Goose, to the younger guys, and then me and Cass.

Near midnight, Riker stood. "Silence!" he ordered.

Instant silence fell.

"You sure about this, Slice?" Riker asked.

"Positive," Slice answered.

I squinted, clueless.

"And you don't care, Goose?"

"Nope."

Riker stared at Drifter and his eyes chilled.

Slice and his twin exchanged glances. Their mood dampened a little, which really piqued my curiosity.

"I guess that's a no for us working together, bro," Drifter said glumly.

No one responded and I wanted the details *now*. Riker walked to where the garment bag lay over the back of a chair, picked it up, and unzipped it. He revealed a leather cut, similar to mine. As he drew closer, I saw a patch with the word, 'President.' On the opposite side, a name—Slice.

My hands flew to my mouth.

Slice tipped his mouth into a half-grin. "In three weeks, we're moving back to Corpus, sweetheart. I know how much you miss Daria and Lennon. Although," he added quickly, "we're not returning for them."

I'm not sure if I screamed louder or Mom.

"Riker offered me the chance to build a new chapter in your hometown, Effie. He and Outlaw worked out a deal. Red Rum will be on one side of Corpus and the Death Dwellers on the other. We have a partnership in the works, which will be beneficial to both clubs."

"This better fucking work," Riker growled.

"Bacán praised Slice," Ziggy said, referring to his chapter's president. "*And* Ophelia likes his woman. It will work. Have faith in your dude."

Riker ignored the Death Dweller. Not that I was surprised. He was even surlier than Cash and ruder than anyone I'd ever met. He scowled at Slice. "Your profits don't belong to the fucking chapter until you repay me the hundred grand I paid for your bounty. Got me?"

"Yes," Slice said calmly, then caressed my cheek, his tender look entrancing me. "Are you fine with this, Effie?"

I nodded, dazed, unable to believe all my dreams were coming true.

Searching my face, Slice continued. "I wanted Drifter to serve dual roles as enforcer and Vice President, Desmond the Road Captain, Dolph Sergeant-at-Arms, and Raider the Treasurer."

Riker smirked.

Slice and Drifter exchanged another miserable glance.

Once Riker turned the back of the cut toward us, I read the top and bottom rockers with misty eyes. In between Red Rum MC and Corpus Christi, the club's emblem stood out.

Riker nodded to Slice's denim cut. Goose walked over and took possession of it once Slice took it off.

"You still need a secretary, Slice," Riker said, watching as Slice donned the leather. "Once the membership grows, I expect democratic elections. Understand?"

Slice nodded.

Riker crooked his finger at Drifter. "You sure about this? Slice's club is starting from the ground up."

"Positive, Prez," Drifter said without hesitation.

Smiling, I leaned into Slice and sighed when he placed his arm around my waist.

"You won't regret this Riker," Goose said, puffing his chest out.

"Just because I've appointed you," Riker went on as if Goose hadn't spoken, "none of you motherfuckers should expect to return to your positions if you're shit officers or if you fuck up. Understand?"

"We do," Slice answered, tension humming through his strong body.

"You got two years, motherfucker," Riker said. He looked at Drifter. "I'm going to miss you, boy," he admitted, and walked out.

"You're moving home, Effie!" Mom cried.

"Yeah, Mom," I responded, only having eyes for Slice.

He bent his head and brushed his lips over mine. "You happy, babe?"

"More than words can express, my love," I murmured, standing on my tiptoes to kiss him back.

In that moment, only he and I existed, and I knew without a doubt that he was who I was meant to spend the rest of my life with.

Mom's voice broke through our cocoon of love and happiness.

"Don't forget, Effie. We have six months to prepare for the next Motorcycles, Mobsters, and Mayhem Book Signing."

THE END

Country Girl by Luke Bryant
Little Bitty by Alan Jackson
A Bar Song by Shaboozey
Buckle Bunny by Tanner Adell
Smile by Florida Georgia Line
Tennessee Whiskey by Chris Stapleton
Honky Tonk Badonkadonk by Trace Adkins
Fancy Like by Walker Hayes
For the Streets by RVSHVD
Forever and Ever Amen by Randy Travis

Thank you for reading Bounty.
If you enjoyed it, please consider leaving a review at your point of purchase and on Goodreads. It means a lot to me to hear what you think. You can also check out other books in the series here: Mayhem Makers
Website: https://katckelly.com

Email: katkelwriter@outlook.com

Snail mail: 24200 Southwest Freeway, Suite 402, Box #353, Rosenberg, TX 77471

Amazon Author Page: https://sqr.co/Follow-Kat-on-Amazon/
Website: https://www.katckelly.com

Dedicated Series Website:
https://deathdwellersmc.com
Facebook:
https://www.facebook.com/kathryn.kelly.336717
Twitter: https://twitter.com/katkelwriter
Blog: http://kathrynkellyauthor.blogspot.com
Pinterest:
http://www.pinterest.com/kathrynkelly336/
Goodreads:
https://www.goodreads.com/author/show/7422779.
Kathryn_Kelly
Instagram: https://www.instagram.com/katkelwriter/
YouTube: https://sqr.co/Kat-on-YouTube/

First and foremost, I want to thank Sapphire Knight. Without your amazing energy and unwavering encouragement, this wouldn't be possible. I'm thrilled to be a part of the Mayhem Maker world and in the company of so many talented authors.

Clarise Tan, you are the best! Thank you so much for your vision and for sharing your talent.

Tasha Hooks, thank you for cheering me on and believing in me.

Finally, to my readers, I cannot thank you enough for wanting to read what I write. Your support inspires me even when I'm at my lowest and my depression is getting the best of me. Without you, I couldn't continue doing what I love.

<u>Mayhem Makers</u>
Bounty

<u>Royal Bastards MC</u>
One Night with a Biker

<u>Death Dwellers MC Legacy</u>
Reckless
Restless
Relentless
Ruthless
Remorseless
Rampage
Revenge

<u>Cocky Hero Club</u>
Savage Suit

Death Dwellers MC
Misled
Misappropriate
Misunderstood
Misdeeds
Misbehavior
Misjudged
Misguided
Misalliance
Misconduct
A Very Christopher Christmas
Misfit
Mistrust
USA Today Review

Misgivings
An Outlaw Valentine
Misrule
Death Dwellers: The Complete Set
Outlaw's Dictionary

Phoenix Rising Rock Band
Inferno
Incendiary
Scorched
Inflame

Dirty Boy Studios
Dirty Boy

Single Titles
Captivated
All My Tomorrows
The Enforcers' Revenge co-written with Emma James
Sexy Santa

Anthologies
Pink: Hot 'N Sexy for a cure: The Books for Boobies 2015
Anthology
When Clubs Collide
Desire Me
The Marriage Monologues – Forever A Dark Obsession
Anthology
Sexy Santa – All I Want For Christmas Anthology

Red Stiletto – Call My Bluff Anthology Hazel & Grayson –
Brothers Grimm Fairytales: An Erotic Anthology
Barebacked – Game Player Anthology
Breakfast & Bedlam – Happily Ever After Anthology
How Innocent My Love – Secrets of Me Anthology
Misconstrued - Forever His Ride Or Die Anthology
My One and Only – Goodbye Doesn't Mean Forever Anthology
Gods & Goddesses – Wicked Realms Anthology
Ignite - My Perfect Pleasure Anthology
Last Chance To Call You Mine
House of Secrets

Writing as Leslie Ferdinand
Wicked Allure
Picture Perfect
Forty Minutes to Disaster - Down In The Dirt Magazine

**Writing as Christine Holden (Mother-Daughter Team
Shirley Ferdinand and Leslie Ferdinand)**
A Time For Us
Patterns of Love
Bedazzled
A Hitch In Time
Dearest Beloved
Een toegewijde dienaar - Dearest Beloved - Audax Publishing
Amsterdam

Kathryn C. Kelly is a New Orleans native who has called southeast Texas home since 2005. She had intended to travel the world but always return to her beloved New Orleans. Hurricane Katrina had other plans. She is the mother of three beautiful daughters and the daughter of one gorgeous mother whose footsteps she followed in by becoming a writer.

Kathryn is the former owner and editor of Inside Rose Rich Magazine. She and her mother have been published by Jove Books as Christine Holden. The books have long been out of print but they got the rights back to the five novels and have plans to re-release them soon.

Kathryn is a cancer survivor. In 2010, she felt a small lump in her breast. In 2015, at the urging of her mother, she went in for her bi-yearly mammogram and was diagnosed with Stage 2b/3a HER2 positive breast cancer. On November 30, 2016, she rang the bell. During her treatment, she was also diagnosed with Li-Fraumeni Syndrome.

She is hard at work on her next book.

In her head, she is a biker babe with a Harley in her garage, waiting for her to hit the road. In reality, she has yet to hop on a bike and ride. She loves Cards Against Humanity, has strong opinions that she keeps to herself, must take her time when she talks in public so nothing untoward pops out, and always strives to see the best in people and in life.

www.ingramcontent.com/pod-product-compliance
Lightning Source LLC
Chambersburg PA
CBHW060351310726
48976CB00003B/783